D0594229

NEW CENTURY READERS

A Roald Dahl Selection

Roald Dahl

Notes: George Kulbacki

Longman

Edinburgh Gate, Harlow
Essex

Pearson Education Limited
Edinburgh Gate
Harlow
Essex
CM20 2JE
England

'The Man from the South', 'Lamb to the Slaughter', 'Galloping
Foxley', 'Skin' and 'The Ratcatcher' are from *Someone Like You,*
originally published by Secker and Warburg Ltd in 1954 and
re-published by Michael Joseph Ltd in 1961. 'The Landlady', 'The
Champion of the World' and 'Mrs Bixby and the Colonel's Coat' are
from *Kiss Kiss* first published by Michael Joseph Ltd in 1960

This collection first published by Longman Group Ltd in association
with Michael Joseph 1960, 1981, a division of Penguin Books Ltd
© 1948, 1949, 1950, 1952, 1953, 1959, 1960 by Roald Dahl
We are grateful to Jonathan Cape Ltd for permission to reproduce
'The Hitchhiker' from *The Wonderful Story of Henry Sugar*

This educational edition first published 2000
Editorial notes © Pearson Education Limited 2000
Seventh impression 2005

ISBN: 0582 43449 1

Printed in China
GCC/07

The Publisher's policy is to use paper manufactured from sustainable
forests.

Contents

Introduction

About the author

Roald Dahl was born in Llandaff, South Wales in 1916. The background to his arrival in the world, and the events surrounding his early childhood, are almost as colourful, eventful and intriguing as the plot of one of his own stories.

Roald Dahl's Norwegian father, Harald Dahl, a successful entrepreneur, had emigrated to South Wales in the 1880s. Tragically Harald's first wife Marie died in 1907 leaving him with a daughter Ellen, aged four, and a son Louis, aged one. On returning to Norway for a holiday Harald met Sofie Magdalene Hesselberg and they married in 1911. Harald and Sofie settled in Llandaff, where over the next six years they had five children: Astri, Alfhild, Roald, Else and Asta. Again tragedy struck the Dahl family when Astri died of appendicitis in 1920. Two months later a heartbroken Harald, who allegedly never really recovered from the death of his beloved daughter, died from pneumonia.

In his will Harald requested that his children be educated in English schools, which were considered to be the best in the world at that time. Sofie Dahl eventually fulfilled the dying wishes of her husband and her son Roald embarked on an education that was to be a rich source of inspiration for much of his autobiographical and fictional writing.

To begin with the young Roald Dahl attended Llandaff Cathedral School for two years, but was withdrawn by his mother after he received a savage beating at the hands of the headmaster. From the age of nine Dahl attended St Peter's Preparatory School, Weston-super-Mare, before going on to the disciplined environment of Repton, a public school in Derbyshire, at 13. Despite his sporting prowess, he remembered his time at Repton without great affection, as it was characterised by violence and corporal punishment administered by older boys.

On leaving Repton in 1934 Roald Dahl went to work for the Shell Oil Company in London and East Africa. In 1939, at the outset of the Second World War, he trained as a fighter pilot, before serving in Kenya, Iraq and Egypt. In 1940 he crash-landed his Gloster Gladiator in the Libyan desert, sustaining horrific injuries to his face. Fortunately he made a remarkable recovery after spending several months in the military hospital at Alexandria, Egypt. He was later to return to flying and served with great courage and skill in Greece, before being invalided home in 1941 as a result of the blackouts and headaches which were the legacy of his earlier accident.

By 1942 Roald Dahl had been posted to Washington DC as air attaché. One of his jobs was to gather intelligence and spy on famous people. It was during this posting that he came into contact with the novelist C.S. Forester who asked Dahl to describe his recollections of flying so he could write about them. Dahl decided that it would be easier to put his ideas down in writing himself. It was in 1942 that Roald Dahl had his first short story published, 'Shot Down Over Libya', in the highly regarded *Saturday Evening Post*. His first book, a children's story, was published in 1943 and was called *Walt Disney: The Gremlins (A Royal Air Force Story By Flight Lieutenant Roald Dahl)*. Walt Disney was highly impressed with Dahl's talent and recognised his obvious potential as a writer of children's stories. Despite Disney's plans to make *Gremlins* into a film, the project was never completed. Dahl's first-hand experience of flying, and the folklore surrounding it, was the basis for much of his earliest writing, but it also emerges in his later work. Some of his best known children's stories such as *The BFG* and *James and the Giant Peach* involve taking the central character on magical flights.

It was around this time that Dahl secured the services of the literary agent, Ann Watkins, who arranged for his stories to be published on a regular basis in American magazines. Dahl's first novel, *Sometime Never*, which expressed his anxieties about nuclear war, was unsuccessfully published in 1948. Despite this early set back, Roald Dahl's varied and successful writing career had begun.

After the Second World War, Roald Dahl spent his time travelling between England and New York City, a place which held a fascination for him and which he romanticised in *James and the Giant Peach*. When in England Dahl lived with his mother Sofie in Amersham, Buckinghamshire trying to establish his reputation as a writer and having limited success with his short stories. It was on one of his visits to New York, in 1951, that Dahl attended a party held by Lillian Hellman, where he was introduced to the famous actress Patricia Neal who was 10 years his junior. Although he initially ignored her, Dahl then asked Neal out to dinner. Despite the reservations of Patricia Neal's close friends, who found Dahl aloof, the couple were married in July 1953. The couple went on to have five children – Olivia, Tessa, Theo, Ophelia and Lucy. Despite enduring many personal tragedies together, including Neal's series of strokes in 1965, the couple divorced in 1983. On 17 November 1983 Dahl married Felicity Crossland.

As far as writing was concerned, Dahl's lucky break came in 1952 when he attracted the attentions of the publisher Alfred Knopf, who was highly impressed with the quality of Dahl's work. Although Knopf's colleagues advised him not to take on Dahl, as there was little prospect of a novel, Knopf published *Someone Like You* in 1953. It was this collection of short stories that established Dahl's reputation as a skilled and highly original writer of adult fiction.

Despite this early recognition as a gifted writer of adult fiction and short stories, it is probably as a writer for young children that Roald Dahl is best remembered. Many of his children's stories continue to entertain and enchant the public, not only in their written form, but also through film and stage productions. In many of the short stories in this selection, the reader is brought face-to-face for the first time with many of the ideas and characters that eventually surface in Dahl's more widely known children's works.

The breadth and range of Roald Dahl's children's writing is well known and has been acknowledged by the numerous writing awards he has received throughout his distinguished career. Sadly he died in November 1990, but the popularity of his books has continued to increase, partly as a result of the many memorable film and stage productions that have been based on his stories. Above all else, it is possibly Dahl's undeniable genius and skilful imagination that is responsible for the continued worldwide appeal of his writing. Whatever the reasons for the obvious success of his writing, Dahl certainly hit upon a winning formula. His mischievous spirit, quick wit and love of the bizarre cannot fail to captivate and enchant both adult and younger readers alike.

Setting the scene
Man from the South
In this story we are introduced to one of Roald Dahl's true passions in life – gambling. The reader is soon shocked to witness the extent the 'oldish man' is prepared to go to satisfy his desire to place outrageous bets. The stakes are high, although the possibility of physical deformity does not deter the reckless, young American soldier. Throughout the story the reader has the uneasy feeling that the 'oldish man' is not merely satisfying a need to gamble but is also gratifying a sadistic inclination for cruelty. It is disturbing that the 'oldish man' has allowed his own wife to experience pain and disfigurement in the pursuit of his hobby.

4

Lamb to the Slaughter

This story initially explores the collapse of what appears to be a perfect relationship. The breakdown of the marriage between Mary and Patrick Maloney is caused by Patrick's unfaithfulness. Typically, Dahl turns traditional roles upside down, with the victim becoming an impulsive murderer. A pregnant and devoted housewife is pushed over an emotional precipice and kills her unfaithful husband. Justice is further served against the male sex through Mary's ability to foil the embarrassing murder investigation of her husband's police colleagues. According to his wife, Patricia Neal, Dahl got the idea while dining with the writer of the James Bond stories, Ian Fleming. Apparently Dahl, to the acute embarrassment of Patricia, interrogated the cook as to the possibilities of murder with an item from a freezer which, at the time, was a very modern appliance.

The Landlady

An apparent belief that the 'weaker sex' is capable of extra-ordinary cruelty is developed further in 'The Landlady', which also reflects his fascination for the grotesque without the need for explicit scenes of horror. It is hard to believe that Billy Weaver's small, neat and apparently hospitable landlady is a sadistic serial killer who preys on unattached and attractive young men. This is a true tale of mystery and suspense, which is only solved in the imagination of the reader. This story is possibly one of Dahl's most skilful, as his use of subtle hints and clues tantalises the reader through to the disturbing ending.

Champion of the World

Roald Dahl's own inclination for danger and risk-taking is apparent in this story. His fondness for the English countryside, its way of life and colourful characters are also clear and are cleverly brought to life with vivid descriptions. Dahl's first-hand knowledge of poaching is also cleverly utilised. Despite Claud's disregard for the law in stealing the pheasants, we somehow feel that justice is served on the repulsive Mr Victor Hazel.

Galloping Foxley

Cruelty, and the pleasure and pain it brings, is again a key feature of 'Galloping Foxley'. We are witnesses to the painful experiences of a young school boy at the hands of his cruel tormentor. How far William Perkins' own experiences mirror those of the writer is not certain, although from Dahl's autobiographical work corporal punishment, administered by one boy to another, was a routine part of daily life at Repton. Sadly, Perkins and the reader are denied a satisfying revenge, despite the skilful ending.

Mrs Bixby and the Colonel's Coat

This story again displays the writer's already established mistrust of women which often sees them employ devious methods in gaining the upper hand in the battle of the sexes. Here Roald Dahl explores each sex's capacity for cheating on the other. There is an uncomfortable tension from the moment the unfaithful Mrs Bixby receives her troublesome gift. Her frustration at not being able to possess the incredible mink coat is cleverly stopped from boiling over at the end of the story, even when she comes face-to-face with her husband's mistress.

Skin

Originally entitled 'A Picture for Drioli', this story is set in post-war Paris in 1946. The impoverished tattoo artist, Drioli, is forced to sell the picture of his wife that his famous artist friend, Soutine, tattooed on his back 30 years previously. The story is a sad reflection on the lengths corrupt art dealers will go to in pursuing rare and valuable paintings. The ending throws up a range of nightmarish possibilities. This story is particularly poignant in the light of Dahl's extensive modern art collection and his enthusiastic love of painting fostered by his artist friend Matthew Smith in the 1940s.

The Ratcatcher

This story, which originally featured in the collection of short stories loosely grouped together under the title *Claud's Dog*, makes up for what it lacks in charm with a deeply disturbing portrayal of the crueller side of country life. Dahl dispels any romantic notions of country life offered in 'The Champion of the World'. Originally rejected by *The New Yorker* in 1952 for its unpleasant and shocking violence, 'The Ratcatcher' was eventually published in *Someone Like You* in 1953.

The Hitchhiker

Very rarely do Dahl's stories have a happy ending, but this story breaks the mould, leaving the reader feeling that all is well with the world. Despite our initial reservations about the devious and crafty hitchhiker he is eventually seen as something of a hero. By the end of the story he is a Robin Hood-type figure, fleecing the rich and undermining the pompous and overbearing traffic policeman. Once again, as in 'The Champion of the World', breaking the law is justified if the situation rights a wrong.

The thoughtfully crafted narratives in this selection are excellent examples of the art of short story writing. Each one has a carefully developed plot, interesting and unusual characters, lively dialogue and careful descriptions which establish the appropriate atmosphere without losing the interest of the reader with unnecessary detail. The originality of the ideas alone is enough to maintain the interest of even the most reluctant reader.

Main themes

Roald Dahl's short stories, whilst not having reached the wider audience of much of his children's writing, still contain those elements of excitement, fantasy and adventure for which he is famous. The stories in this selection are particularly appealing for their original and imaginative use of language, and the simple, almost effortless, manner in which ideas and events are conveyed. As with his writing for young children, Roald Dahl's intuitive feel for the rhythms of the English language make these narratives a pleasure to read.

Roald Dahl's first-hand experiences of the English public school system, along with his playful observations during his many travels and adventures, are often the direct source and inspiration for this selection of short stories. The cruelty of the English public school system, with its harsh discipline and corporal punishment, is well documented in Dahl's autobiographical book *Boy*, published in 1984. It is in the short story 'Galloping Foxley', however, published in 1953 in *Someone Like You*, that many of his strongest school day memories of Repton surface for the first time.

Interests, events and friendships formed in Dahl's early life provide the inspiration for other stories. Many of his tales of country life featuring the character Claud are based on one of his gambling associates, the Amersham butcher Claud Taylor, who helped Dahl train greyhounds immediately after the Second World War. Taylor also coached Dahl in the arts of tickling trout and poaching. It was only when *Danny the Champion of the World* was published in 1975 that Dahl's painstaking record of his rural existence during his misspent post-war years really bore fruit. The short story, 'The Champion of the World' possesses much of the charm and atmosphere of the later children's story, as well as many of the same ideas.

Roald Dahl has often been praised for his brilliant imagination, range of ideas and sense of mischief. However, beneath the subtle humour, there is an underlying fascination with cruelty and the macabre. In many of his stories he explores the darker side of human nature, occasionally giving apparently normal people the capacity for violent and unnatural behaviour.

Language and style

Very often short stories begin with a dramatic and powerful opening to grab the reader's attention from the start. Many of the stories in this selection, however, begin with a description of a commonplace setting, an ordinary character and a calm, routine existence. First appearances are often deceptive and lull the reader into a false sense of security. Everything appears normal. However, it does not take long for Dahl to change the atmosphere. When reading 'Lamb to the Slaughter', for instance, it is difficult to imagine how the cosy domestic existence of Mary Maloney can be quickly transformed into the scene of a bizarre murder. Ordinary events and actions, such as travelling to work by train in 'Galloping Foxley', can become the setting for a tale of unbearable and savage physical torment. Through a mixture of clever twists and turns, and unexpected circumstances, Dahl is always able to capture and maintain the reader's interest.

With each new story there is no knowing which way the action will develop. No two stories are the same. Occasionally the plot will unfold by implication, with a series of subtle hints and vague clues as in 'The Landlady'. There is merely an uneasy feeling of something not being quite right.

From time to time Roald Dahl employs a bizarre and unexpected event which shocks the reader, as in 'The Ratcatcher' or 'Lamb to the Slaughter'. Whatever method Dahl employs to capture the reader's attention, shock, revulsion, or a subtle twist in the plot, he always guarantees a well-timed and startling ending. The conclusion to each story in this selection is always memorable and thought-provoking; often lingering in the imagination of the reader for a long time.

The combination of Dahl's extraordinary and ingenious imagination, with his unusual personal encounters and recollections, create a powerful and thought-provoking mixture that ensures that the reader is 'hooked' right to the end of the narrative. At the end of each story the reader is invariably left with a number of strange ideas and intriguing possibilities on which to ponder. The fate of Billy Weaver in 'The Landlady' or the tattoo artist Drioli in 'Skin' can only be guessed at. Part of the pleasure of reading this selection is unravelling the possibilities which Dahl has ingeniously suggested. An explicit description of the nightmarish fates that Dahl had devised for many of his characters in his short stories would have been too horrific for the majority of the readers of the magazines in which they were originally published. In fact, on many occasions, Dahl's taste for death and the macabre had to be considerably watered down to be acceptable to his publishers. The popular 1970s television series *Tales of the Unexpected*, for which Dahl adapted many of his short stories like 'The Landlady', actually constructed the ending for the viewer, so there could be no doubt as to the gruesome destiny of some less fortunate characters. These stories often take the reader on a journey into the darker side of the imagination.

A Roald Dahl Selection

Notes on Man from the South

The beginning of any short story is important as the writer has to immediately capture the attention of the reader. Very often openings involve descriptions of people and places which quickly establish the atmosphere. The tension of this story is soon built up with an unusual twist to the action. It is interesting to compare the relative calm at the start of many of the stories with the shocking nature of the events that follow.

What do you think?
As you read the opening page think about your first impressions. Consider the setting and the atmosphere – how do they make you feel? How is the atmosphere changed? For example:
- Look at the descriptions of the first few paragraphs – what is taking place?
- Does the the introduction of the 'small oldish man' change the mood?
- What might happen in this story?

Questions
Find words and phrases in the text to support your answers to these questions:
1. What are your first impressions of the 'oldish man'?
2. How does the narrator feel about the behaviour of the oldish man?
3. What are the terms of the bet? Do you think they are reasonable?
4. How do the different characters react to the idea of the bet? You should consider the reactions of the American sailor, the narrator and the English girl.
5. How does Roald Dahl build up the tension in the old man's bedroom? What impact does the small black-haired woman have on this scene and the story as a whole?

Further activity
Imagine that you are either the American sailor or the English girl. Write a letter to a friend describing the events of the story. Explain how you feel at the various stages in the action and describe your feelings towards the different characters.

Man from the South

It was getting on towards six o'clock so I thought I'd buy myself a beer and go out and sit in a deckchair by the swimming pool and have a little evening sun.

I went to the bar and got the beer and carried it outside and wandered down the garden towards the pool.

It was a fine garden with lawns and beds of azaleas and tall coconut palms, and the wind was blowing strongly through the tops of the palm trees, making the leaves hiss and crackle as though they were on fire. I could see the clusters of big brown nuts hanging down underneath the leaves.

There were plenty of deck-chairs around the swimming pool and there were white tables and huge brightly coloured umbrellas and sunburned men and women sitting around in bathing suits. In the pool itself there were three or four girls and about a dozen boys, all splashing about and making a lot of noise and throwing a large rubber ball at one another.

I stood watching them. The girls were English girls from the hotel. The boys I didn't know about, but they sounded American, and I thought they were probably naval cadets who'd come ashore from the US naval training vessel which had arrived in harbour that morning.

I went over and sat down under a yellow umbrella where there were four empty seats, and I poured my beer and settled back comfortably with a cigarette.

It was very pleasant sitting there in the sunshine with beer and cigarette. It was pleasant to sit and watch the bathers splashing about in the green water.

The American sailors were getting on nicely with the English girls. They'd reached the stage where they were diving under the water and tipping them up by their legs.

Just then I noticed a small, oldish man walking briskly around the edge of the pool. He was immaculately dressed in a white suit and he walked very quickly with little bouncing strides, pushing himself high up on to his toes with each step. He had on a large creamy Panama hat, and he came bouncing along the side of the pool, looking at the people and the chairs.

He stopped beside me and smiled, showing two rows of very small, uneven teeth, slightly tarnished. I smiled back.

'Excuse pleess, but may I sit here?'

'Certainly,' I said, 'Go ahead.'

He bobbed around to the back of the chair and inspected it for safety, then he sat down and crossed his legs. His white buckskin shoes had little holes punched all over them for ventilation.

'A fine evening,' he said. 'They are all evenings fine here in Jamaica.' I couldn't tell if the accent were Italian or Spanish, but I felt fairly sure he was some sort of a South American. And old too, when you saw him close. Probably around sixty-eight or seventy.

'Yes,' I said. 'It is wonderful here, isn't it.'

'And who, might I ask, are all dese? Dese is no hotel people.' He was pointing at the bathers in the pool.

'I think they're American sailors,' I told him. 'They're Americans who are learning to be sailors.'

'Of course dey are Americans. Who else in de world is going to make as much noise as dat? You are not American no?'

'No,' I said. 'I am not.'

Suddenly one of the American cadets was standing in front of us. He was dripping wet from the pool and one of the English girls was standing there with him.

'Are these chairs taken?' he said.

'No,' I answered.

'Mind if I sit down?'

'Go ahead.'

14

'Thanks,' he said. He had a towel in his hand and when he sat down he unrolled it and produced a pack of cigarettes and a lighter. He offered the cigarettes to the girl and she refused; then he offered them to me and I took one. The little man said, 'Tank you, no but I tink I have a cigar.' He pulled out a crocodile case and got himself a cigar, then he produced a knife which had a small scissors in it and he snipped the end off the cigar.

'Here, let me give you a light.' The American boy held up his lighter.

'Dat will not work in dis wind.'

'Sure it'll work. It always works.'

The little man removed his unlighted cigar from his mouth, cocked his head on one side and looked at the boy.

'*All*-ways?' he said slowly.

'Sure, it never fails. Not with me anyway.'

The little man's head was still cocked over on one side and he was still watching the boy. 'Well, well. So you say dis famous lighter it never fails. Iss dat you say?'

'Sure,' the boy said. 'That's right.' He was about nineteen or twenty with a long freckled face and a rather sharp birdlike nose. His chest was not very sunburned and there were freckles there too, and a few wisps of pale-reddish hair. He was holding the lighter in his right hand, ready to flip the wheel. 'It never fails,' he said, smiling now because he was purposely exaggerating his little boast. 'I promise you it never fails.'

'One momint, pleess.' The hand that held the cigar came up high, palm outward, as though it were stopping traffic. 'Now juss one momint.' He had a curiously soft, toneless voice and he kept looking at the boy all the time.

'Shall we not perhaps make a little bet on dat?' He smiled at the boy. 'Shall we not make a little bet on whether your lighter lights?'

'Sure, I'll bet,' the boy said. 'Why not?'

'You like to bet?'

15

'Sure, I'll always bet.'

The man paused and examined his cigar, and I must say I didn't much like the way he was behaving. It seemed he was already trying to make something out of this, and to embarrass the boy, and at the same time I had the feeling he was relishing a private little secret all his own.

He looked up again at the boy and said slowly. 'I like to bet, too. Why we don't have a good bet on dis ting? A good big bet.'

'Now wait a minute,' the boy said. 'I can't do that. But I'll bet you a quarter. I'll even bet you a dollar, or whatever it is over here – some shillings, I guess.'

The little man waved his hand again. 'Listen to me. Now we have some fun. We make a bet. Den we go up to my room here in de hotel where iss no wind and I bet you you cannot light dis famous lighter of yours ten times running without missing once.'

'I'll bet I can,' the boy said.

'All right. Good. We make a bet, yes?'

'Sure, I'll bet you a buck.'

'No, no. I make you a very good bet. I am rich man and I am sporting man also. Listen to me. Outside de hotel iss my car. Iss very fine car. American car from your country. Cadillac –'

'Hey, now. Wait a minute.' The boy leaned back in his deck-chair and he laughed. 'I can't put up that sort of property. This is crazy.'

'Not crazy at all. You strike lighter successfully ten times running and Cadillac is yours. You like to have dis Cadillac, yes?'

'Sure, I'd like to have a Cadillac.' The boy was still grinning.

'All right. Fine. We make a bet and I put up my Cadillac.'

'And what do I put up?'

The little man carefully removed the red band from his still unlighted cigar. 'I never ask you, my friend, to bet something you cannot afford. You understand?'

Then what do I bet?'

'I make it very easy for you, yes?'

'Okay. You make it easy.'

'Some small ting you can afford to give away, and if you did happen to lose it you would not feel too bad. Right?'

'Such as what?'

'Such as, perhaps, de little finger on your left hand.'

'My *what*?' The boy stopped grinning.

'Yes. Why not? You win, you take de car. You looss, I take de finger.'

'I don't get it. How d'you mean, you take the finger?'

'I chop it off.'

'Jumping jeepers. That's a crazy bet. I think I'll just make it a dollar.'

The little man leaned back, spread out his hands palms upwards and gave a tiny contemptuous shrug of the shoulders. 'Well, well, well,' he said. 'I do not understand. You say it lights but you will not bet. Den we forget it, yes?'

The boy sat quite still, staring at the bathers in the pool. Then he remembered suddenly he hadn't lighted his cigarette. He put it between his lips, cupped his hands around the lighter and flipped the wheel. The wick lighted and burned with a small, steady, yellow flame and the way he held his hands the wind didn't get to it at all.

'Could I have a light, too?' I said.

'God, I'm sorry, I forgot you didn't have one.'

I held out my hand for the lighter, but he stood up and came over to do it for me.

'Thank you,' I said, and he returned to his seat.

'You having a good time?' I asked.

'Fine,' he answered. 'It's pretty nice here.'

There was a silence then, and I could see that the little man had succeeded in disturbing the boy with his absurd proposal. He was sitting there very still, and it was obvious that a small tension was beginning to build up inside him. Then he started shifting about in his seat, and rubbing his chest, and stroking the back of his neck, and finally he placed both hands on his knees and began tap-tapping with his fingers against the kneecaps. Soon he was tapping with one of his feet as well.

'Now just let me check up on this bet of yours,' he said at last. 'You say we go up to your room and if I make this lighter light ten times running I win a Cadillac. If it misses just once then I forfeit the little finger of my left hand. Is that right?'

'Certainly. Dat is de bet. But I tink you are afraid.'

'What do we do if I lose? Do I have to hold my finger out while you chop it off?'

'Oh, no! Dat would be no good. And you might be tempted to refuse to hold it out. What I should do I should tie one of your hands to de table before we started and I should stand dere with a knife ready to go *chop* de momint your lighter missed.'

'What year is the Cadillac?' the boy asked.

'Excuse. I not understand.'

'What year – how old is the Cadillac?'

'Ah! How old? Yes. It is last year. Quite new car. But I see you are not betting man. Americans never are.'

The boy paused for just a moment and he glanced first at the English girl, then at me. 'Yes,' he said sharply. 'I'll bet you.'

'Good!' The little man clapped his hands together quietly, once. 'Fine,' he said. 'We do it now. And you, sir,' he turned to me, 'you would perhaps be good enough to, what you call it, to – to referee.' He had pale, almost colourless eyes with tiny bright black pupils.

'Well,' I said. 'I think it's a crazy bet. I don't think I like it very much.'

'Nor do I,' said the English girl. It was the first time she'd spoken. 'I think it's a stupid, ridiculous bet.'

'Are you serious about cutting off this boy's finger if he loses?' I said.

18

'Certainly I am. Also about giving him Cadillac if he win. Come now. We go to my room.'

He stood up. 'You like to put on some clothes first?' he said.

'No,' the boy answered. 'I'll come like this.' Then he turned to me. 'I'd consider it a favour if you'd come along and referee.'

'All right,' I said. 'I'll come along, but I don't like the bet.'

'You come too,' he said to the girl. 'You come and watch.'

The little man led the way back through the garden to the hotel. He was animated now, and excited, and that seemed to make him bounce up higher than ever on his toes as he walked along.

'I live in annexe,' he said. 'You like to see car first? Iss just here.'

He took us to where we could see the front driveway of the hotel and he stopped and pointed to a sleek pale-green Cadillac parked close by.

'Dere she iss. De green one. You like?'

'Say, that's a nice car,' the boy said.

'All right. Now we go up and see if you can win her.'

We followed him into the annexe and up one flight of stairs. He unlocked his door and we all trooped into what was a large pleasant double bedroom. There was a woman's dressing-gown lying across the bottom of one of the beds.

'First,' he said, 'we 'ave a little Martini.'

The drinks were on a small table in the far corner, all ready to be mixed, and there was a shaker and ice and plenty of glasses. He began to make the Martini, but meanwhile he'd rung the bell and now there was a knock on the door and a coloured maid came in.

'Ah!' he said, putting down the bottle of gin, taking a wallet from his pocket and pulling out a pound note. 'You will do something for me now, pleess.' He gave the maid the pound.

'You keep dat,' he said. 'And now we are going to play a little game in here and I want you to go off and find for me two – no

19

tree tings. I want some nails, I want a hammer, and I want a chopping knife, a butcher's chopping knife which you can borrow from de kitchen. You can get, yes?'

'A *chopping knife*!' The maid opened her eyes wide and clasped her hands in front of her. 'You mean a *real* chopping knife?'

'Yes, yes, of course. Come on now, pleess. You can find dose tings surely for me.'

'Yes, sir, I'll try, sir. Surely I'll try to get them.' And she went.

The little man handed round the Martinis. We stood there and sipped them, the boy with the long freckled face and the pointed nose, bare-bodied except for a pair of faded brown bathing shorts: the English girl, a large-boned fair-haired girl wearing a pale blue bathing suit, who watched the boy over the top of her glass all the time; the little man with the colourless eyes standing there in his immaculate white suit drinking his Martini and looking at the girl in her pale blue bathing dress. I didn't know what to make of it all. The man seemed serious about the bet and he seemed serious about the business of cutting off the finger. But hell, what if the boy lost? Then we'd have to rush him to the hospital in the Cadillac that he hadn't won. That would be a fine thing. Now wouldn't that be a really fine thing? It would be a damn silly unnecessary thing so far as I could see.

'Don't you think this is rather a silly bet?' I said.

'I think it's a fine bet,' the boy answered. He had already downed one large Martini.

'I think it's a stupid, ridiculous bet,' the girl said. 'What'll happen if you lost?'

'It won't matter. Come to think of it, I can't remember ever in my life having had any use for the little finger on my left hand. Here he is.' The boy took hold of the finger. 'Here he is and he hasn't ever done a thing for me yet. So why shouldn't I bet him? I think it's a fine bet.'

20

The little man smiled and picked up the shaker and refilled our glasses.

'Before we begin,' he said, 'I will present to de – to de referee de key of de car.' He produced a car key from his pocket and gave it to me. 'De papers,' he said, 'de owning papers and insurance are in de pocket of de car.'

Then the coloured maid came in again. In one hand she carried a small chopper, the kind used by butchers for chopping meat bones, and in the other a hammer and a bag of nails.

'Good! You get dem all. Tank you, tank you. Now you can go.' He waited until the maid had closed the door, then he put the implements on one of the beds and said, 'Now we prepare ourselves, yes?' And to the boy, 'Help me, pleess, with dis table. We carry it out a little.'

It was the usual kind of hotel writing desk, just a plain rectangular table about four feet by three with a blotting pad, ink, pens and paper. They carried it out into the room away from the wall, and removed the writing things.

'And now,' he said, 'a chair.' He picked up a chair and placed it beside the table. He was very brisk and very animated, like a person organising games at a children's party. 'And now de nails. I must put in de nails.' He fetched the nails and he began to hammer them into the top of the table.

We stood there, the boy, the girl, and I, holding Martinis in our hands, watching the little man at work. We watched him hammer two nails into the table, about six inches apart. He didn't hammer them right home; he allowed a small part of each one to stick up. Then he tested them for firmness with his fingers.

Anyone would think the son of a bitch had done this before, I told myself. He never hesitates. Table, nails, hammer, kitchen chopper. He knows exactly what he needs and how to arrange it.

'And now,' he said, 'all we want is some string.' He found some string. 'All right, at last we are ready. Will you pleess to sit here at de table?' he said to the boy.

The boy put his glass away and sat down.

'Now place de left hand between dese two nails. De nails are only so I can tie your hand in place. All right, good. Now I tie your hand secure to de table – so.'

He wound the string around the boy's wrist, then several times around the wide part of the hand, then he fastened it tight to the nails. He made a good job of it and when he'd finished there wasn't any question about the boy being able to draw his hand away. But he could move his fingers.

'Now pleess, clench de fist, all except for de little finger. You must leave de little finger sticking out, lying on de table.'

'*Ex*-cellent! *Ex*-cellent! Now we are ready. Wid your right hand you manipulate de lighter. But one momint, pleess.'

He skipped over to the bed and picked up the chopper. He came back and stood beside the table with the chopper in his hand.

'We are all ready?' he said. 'Mister referee, you must say to begin.'

The English girl was standing there in her pale blue bathing costume right behind the boy's chair. She was just standing there, not saying anything. The boy was sitting quite still, holding the lighter in his right hand, looking at the chopper. The little man was looking at me.

'Are you ready?' I asked the boy.

'I'm ready.'

'And you?' to the little man.

'Quite ready,' he said and he lifted the chopper up in the air and held it there about two feet above the boy's finger, ready to chop. The boy watched it, but he didn't flinch and his mouth didn't move at all. He merely raised his eyebrows and frowned.

'All right,' I said. 'Go ahead.'

The boy said, 'Will you please count aloud the number of times I light it.'

'Yes,' I said. 'I'll do that.'

With his thumb he raised the top of the lighter, and again with the thumb he gave the wheel a sharp flick. The flint sparked and the wick caught fire and burned with a small yellow flame.

'One!' I called.

He didn't blow the flame out; he closed the top of the lighter on it and he waited for perhaps five seconds before opening it again.

He flicked the wheel very strongly and once more there was a small flame burning on the wick.

'Two!'

No one else said anything. The boy kept his eyes on the lighter. The little man held the chopper up in the air and he too was watching the lighter.

'Three!'

'Four!'

'Five!'

'Six!'

'Seven!' Obviously it was one of those lighters that worked. The flint gave a big spark and the wick was the right length.

I watched the thumb snapping the top down on to the flame. Then a pause. Then the thumb raising the top once more. This was an all-thumb operation. The thumb did everything. I took a breath, ready to say eight. The thumb flicked the wheel. The flint sparked. The little flame appeared.

'Eight!' I said, and as I said it the door opened. We all turned and we saw a woman standing in the doorway, a small, black-haired woman, rather old, who stood there for about two seconds then rushed forward, shouting, 'Carlos! Carlos!' She grabbed his wrist, took the chopper from him, threw it on the bed, took hold of the little man by the lapels of his white suit and began shaking him very vigorously, talking to him fast and

23

loud and fiercely all the time in some Spanish-sounding language. She shook him so fast you couldn't see him any more. He became a faint, misty, quickly moving outline, like the spokes of a turning wheel.

Then she slowed down and the little man came into view again and she hauled him across the room and pushed him backwards on to one of the beds. He sat on the edge of it blinking his eyes and testing his head to see if it would still turn on his neck.

'I am sorry,' the woman said. 'I am so terribly sorry that this should happen.' She spoke almost perfect English.

'It is too bad,' she went on. 'I suppose it is really my fault. For ten minutes I leave him alone to go and have my hair washed and I come back and he is at it again.' She looked sorry and deeply concerned.

The boy was untying his hand from the table. The English girl and I stood there and said nothing.

'He is a menace,' the woman said. 'Down where we live at home he has taken altogether forty-seven fingers from different people, and he has lost eleven cars. In the end they threatened to have him put away somewhere. That's why I brought him up here.'

'We were only having a little bet,' mumbled the little man from the bed.

'I suppose he bet you a car,' the woman said.

'Yes,' the boy answered. 'A Cadillac.'

'He has no car. It's mine. And that makes it worse,' she said, 'that he should bet you when he has nothing to bet with. I am ashamed and very sorry about it all.' She seemed an awfully nice woman.

'Well,' I said, 'then here's the key of your car.' I put it on the table.

'We were only having a little bet,' mumbled the little man. 'He hasn't anything left to bet with,' the woman said. 'He hasn't a

24

thing in the world. Not a thing. As a matter of fact I myself won it all from him a long while ago. It took time, a lot of time, and it was hard work, but I won it all in the end.' She looked up at the boy and she smiled, a slow sad smile, and she came over and put out a hand to take the key from the table.

I can see it now, that hand of hers; it had only one finger on it, and a thumb.

Notes on Lamb to the Slaughter

By now you may realise that things are not always as they seem in Roald Dahl's short stories. Impressions of people and places at the beginning of a story, and the atmosphere they generate, can quickly be changed by dramatic and unexpected events. In 'Lamb to the Slaughter' it is difficult to imagine how Dahl can involve his fascination for the bizarre and violent in the apparently peaceful and ordinary life of Mary Maloney.

What do you think?
As you read the beginning of this story think about your first impressions of Mary Maloney and her home. Consider how Roald Dahl changes the reader's attitude towards Mary as the story progresses. Consider:
- What initial impressions do we have of Mary and her relationship with her husband?
- Who do you have the most sympathy for at the end of the story, Mary or Patrick?

Questions
Pick out words, phrases and events in the story to support your answers to these questions:
1. When Patrick Maloney arrives home, what is there in his actions and speech that suggest there is something wrong?
2. Patrick clearly gives Mary some distressing news. What might this news be?
3. How does Mary react to Patrick's news?
4. Describe and explain Mary's actions after Patrick's death.
5. What do you think of the way the police investigate Patrick Maloney's murder?

Further activity
Imagine you are one of the detectives assigned to investigate the murder of Patrick Maloney. Write a report describing your murder investigation. In your report you should include:
- a description of the crime scene
- statements from Mary Maloney and the shopkeeper
- an explanation of what you think might have happened.

Lamb to the Slaughter

The room was warm and clean, the curtains drawn, the two table lamps alight – hers and the one by the empty chair opposite. On the sideboard behind her, two tall glasses, soda water, whisky. Fresh ice cubes in the Thermos bucket.

Mary Maloney was waiting for her husband to come home from work.

Now and again she would glance up at the clock, but without anxiety, merely to please herself with the thought that each minute gone by made it nearer the time when he would come. There was a slow smiling air about her, and about everything she did. The drop of the head as she bent over her sewing was curiously tranquil. Her skin – for this was her sixth month with child – had acquired a wonderful translucent quality, the mouth was soft, and the eyes, with their new placid look, seemed larger, darker than before.

When the clock said ten minutes to five, she began to listen, and a few moments later, punctually as always, she heard the tyres on the gravel outside, and the car door slamming, the footsteps passing the window, the key turning in the lock. She laid aside her sewing, stood up, and went forward to kiss him as he came in.

'Hullo, darling,' she said.

'Hullo,' he answered.

She took his coat and hung it in the closet. Then she walked over and made the drinks, a strongish one for him, a weak one for herself; and soon she was back again in her chair with the sewing, and he in the other, opposite, holding the tall glass with both his hands, rocking it so the ice cubes tinkled against the side.

For her, this was always a blissful time of day. She knew he didn't want to speak much until the first drink was finished, and she, on her side, was content to sit quietly, enjoying his company after the long hours alone in the house. She loved to luxuriate in the presence of this man, and to feel almost as a sunbather feels the sun that warm male glow that came out of him to her when they were alone together. She loved him for the way he sat loosely in a chair, for the way he came in a door, or moved slowly across the room with long strides. She loved the intent, far look in his eyes when they rested on her, the funny shape of the mouth, and especially the way he remained silent about his tiredness, sitting still with himself until the whisky had taken some of it away.

'Tired, darling?'

'Yes,' he said. 'I'm tired.' And as he spoke, he did an unusual thing. He lifted his glass and drained it in one swallow although there was still half of it, at least half of it, left. She wasn't really watching him but she knew what he had done because she heard the ice cubes falling back against the bottom of the empty glass when he lowered his arm. He paused a moment, leaning forward in the chair, then he got up and went slowly over to fetch himself another.

'I'll get it!' she cried, jumping up.

'Sit down,' he said.

When he came back, she noticed that the new drink was dark amber with the quantity of whisky in it.

'Darling, shall I get your slippers?'

'No.'

She watched him as he began to sip the dark yellow drink, and she could see little oily swirls in the liquid because it was so strong.

'I think it's a shame,' she said, 'that when a policeman gets to be as senior as you, they keep him walking about on his feet all day long.'

He didn't answer, so she bent her head again and went on with her sewing; but each time he lifted the drink to his lips, she heard the ice cubes clinking against the side of the glass.

'Darling,' she said. 'Would you like me to get you some cheese? I haven't made any supper because it's Thursday.'

'No,' he said.

'If you're too tired to eat out,' she went on, 'it's still not too late. There's plenty of meat and stuff in the freezer, and you can have it right here and not even move out of the chair.'

Her eyes waited on him for an answer, a smile, a little nod, but he made no sign.

'Anyway,' she went on, 'I'll get you some cheese and crackers first.'

'I don't want it,' he said.

She moved uneasily in her chair, the large eyes still watching his face. 'But you *must* have supper. I can easily do it here. I'd like to do it. We can have lamb chops. Or pork. Anything you want. Everything's in the freezer.'

'Forget it,' he said.

'But, darling, you *must* eat! I'll fix it anyway, and then you can have it or not, as you like.'

She stood up and placed her sewing on the table by the lamp.

'Sit down,' he said. 'Just for a minute, sit down.'

It wasn't till then that she began to get frightened.

'Go on,' he said. 'Sit down.'

She lowered herself back slowly into the chair, watching him all the time with those large, bewildered eyes. He had finished the second drink and was staring down into the glass, frowning.

'Listen,' he said, 'I've got something to tell you.'

'What is it, darling? What's the matter?'

He had become absolutely motionless, and he kept his head down so that the light from the lamp beside him fell across the upper part of his face, leaving the chin and mouth in shadow. She noticed there was a little muscle moving near the corner of his left eye.

29

'This is going to be a bit of a shock to you, I'm afraid,' he said. 'But I've thought about it a good deal and I've decided the only thing to do is tell you right away. I hope you won't blame me too much.'

And he told her. It didn't take long, four or five minutes at most, and she sat very still through it all, watching him with a kind of dazed horror as he went further and further away from her with each word.

'So there it is,' he added. 'And I know it's kind of a bad time to be telling you, but there simply wasn't any other way. Of course I'll give you money and see you're looked after. But there needn't really be any fuss. I hope not anyway. It wouldn't be very good for my job.'

Her first instinct was not to believe any of it, to reject it all. It occurred to her that perhaps he hadn't even spoken, that she herself had imagined the whole thing. Maybe, if she went about her business and acted as though she hadn't been listening, then later, when she sort of woke up again, she might find none of it had ever happened.

'I'll get the supper,' she managed to whisper, and this time he didn't stop her.

When she walked across the room she couldn't feel her feet touching the floor. She couldn't feel anything at all – except a slight nausea and a desire to vomit. Everything was automatic now – down the stairs to the cellar, the light switch, the deep freeze, the hand inside the cabinet taking hold of the first object it met. She lifted it out, and looked at it. It was wrapped in paper, so she took off the paper and looked at it again.

A leg of lamb.

All right then, they would have lamb for supper. She carried it upstairs, holding the thin bone-end of it with both her hands, and as she went through the living-room, she saw him standing over by the window with his back to her, and she stopped.

'For God's sake,' he said, hearing her, but not turning round, 'Don't make supper for me. I'm going out.'

At that point, Mary Maloney simply walked up behind him and without any pause she swung the big frozen leg of lamb high in the air and brought it down as hard as she could on the back of his bead.

She might just as well have hit him with a steel club.

She stepped back a pace, waiting, and the funny thing was that he remained standing there for at least four or five seconds, gently swaying. Then he crashed to the carpet.

The violence of the crash, the noise, the small table overturning, helped bring her out of the shock. She came out slowly, feeling cold and surprised, and she stood for a while blinking at the body, still holding the ridiculous piece of meat tight with both hands.

All right, she told herself. So I've killed him.

It was extraordinary, now, how clear her mind became all of a sudden. She began thinking very fast. As the wife of a detective, she knew quite well what the penalty would be. That was fine. It made no difference to her. In fact, it would be a relief. On the other hand, what about the child? What were the laws about murderers with unborn children? Did they kill them both – mother and child? Or did they wait until the tenth month? What did they do?

Mary Maloney didn't know. And she certainly wasn't prepared to take a chance.

She carried the meat into the kitchen, placed it in a pan, turned the oven on high, and shoved it inside. Then she washed her hands and ran upstairs to the bedroom. She sat down before the mirror, tidied her face, touched up her lips and face. She tried a smile. It came out rather peculiar. She tried again.

'Hullo Sam,' she said brightly, aloud.

The voice sounded peculiar too.

'I want some potatoes please, Sam. Yes, and I think a can of peas.'

That was better. Both the smile and the voice were coming out better now. She rehearsed it several times more. Then she ran downstairs, took her coat, went out the back door, down the garden, into the street.

It wasn't six o'clock yet and the lights were still on in the grocery shop.

'Hullo Sam,' she said brightly, smiling at the man behind the counter.

'Why, good evening, Mrs Maloney. How're you?'

'I want some potatoes please, Sam. Yes, and I think a can of peas.'

The man turned and reached up behind him on the shelf for the peas.

'Patrick's decided he's tired and doesn't want to eat out tonight,' she told him. 'We usually go out Thursdays, you know, and now he's caught me without any vegetables in the house.'

'Then how about meat, Mrs Maloney?'

'No, I've got meat, thanks. I got a nice leg of lamb, from the freezer.'

'Oh.'

'I don't much like cooking it frozen, Sam, but I'm taking a chance on it this time. You think it'll be all right?'

'Personally,' the grocer said, 'I don't believe it makes any difference. You want these Idaho potatoes?'

'Oh yes, that'll be fine. Two of those.'

'Anything else?' The grocer cocked his head on one side, looking at her pleasantly. 'How about afterwards? What you going to give him for afterwards?'

'Well – what would you suggest, Sam?'

The man glanced around his shop. 'How about a nice big slice of cheesecake? I know he likes that.'

'Perfect,' she said. 'He loves it.'

And when it was all wrapped and she had paid, she put on her brightest smile and said, 'Thank you, Sam. Good night.'

'Good night, Mrs Maloney. And thank *you*.'

And now, she told herself as she hurried back, all she was doing now, she was returning home to her husband and he was waiting for his supper; and she must cook it good, and make it as tasty as possible because the poor man was tired; and if, when she entered the house, she happened to find anything unusual, or tragic, or terrible, then naturally it would be a shock and she'd become frantic with grief and horror. Mind you, she wasn't *expecting* to find anything. She was just going home with the vegetables. Mrs Patrick Maloney going home with the vegetables on Thursday evening to cook supper for her husband.

That's the way, she told herself. Do everything right and natural. Keep things absolutely natural and there'll be no need for any acting at all.

Therefore, when she entered the kitchen by the back door, she was humming a little tune to herself and smiling.

'Patrick!' she called. 'How are you, darling?'

She put the parcel down on the table and went through into the living-room; and when she saw him lying there on the floor with his legs doubled up and one arm twisted back underneath his body, it really was rather a shock. All the old love and longing for him welled up inside her, and she ran over to him, knelt down beside him, and began to cry her heart out. It was easy. No acting was necessary.

A few minutes later she got up and went to the phone. She knew the number of the police station, and when the man at the other end answered, she cried to him, 'Quick! Come quick! Patrick's dead!'

'Who's speaking?'

'Mrs Maloney. Mrs Patrick Maloney.'

'You mean Patrick Maloney's dead?'

'I think so,' she sobbed. 'He's lying on the floor and I think he's dead.'

'Be right over,' the man said.

The car came very quickly, and when she opened the front door, two policemen walked in. She knew them both – she knew nearly all the men at that precinct – and she fell right into Jack Noonan's arms, weeping hysterically. He put her gently into a chair, then went over to join the other one, who was called O'Malley, kneeling by the body.

'Is he dead?' she cried.

'I'm afraid he is. What happened?'

Briefly, she told her story about going out to the grocer and coming back to find him on the floor. While she was talking, crying and talking, Noonan discovered a small patch of congealed blood on the dead man's head. He showed it to O'Malley who got up at once and hurried to the phone.

Soon, other men began to come into the house. First a doctor, then two detectives, one of whom she knew by name. Later, a police photographer arrived and took pictures, and a man who knew about fingerprints. There was a great deal of whispering and muttering beside the corpse, and the detectives kept asking her a lot of questions. But they always treated her kindly. She told her story again, this time right from the beginning, when Patrick had come in, and she was sewing, and he was tired, so tired he hadn't wanted to go out for supper. She told how she'd put the meat in the oven – 'it's there now, cooking' – and how she'd slipped out to the grocer for vegetables, and come back to find him lying on the floor.

'Which grocer?' one of the detectives asked.

She told him, and he turned and whispered something to the other detective who immediately went outside into the street.

In fifteen minutes he was back with a page of notes, and there was more whispering, and through her sobbing she heard a few of the whispered phrases – '... acted quite normal ... very cheerful ... wanted to give him a good supper ... peas ... cheesecake ... impossible that she ...'

After a while, the photographer and the doctor departed and two other men came in and took the corpse away on a stretcher. Then the fingerprint man went away. The two detectives remained, and so did the two policemen. They were exceptionally nice to her, and Jack Noonan asked if she wouldn't rather go somewhere else, to her sister's house perhaps, or to his own wife who would take care of her and put her up for the night.

No, she said, She didn't feel she could move even a yard at the moment. Would they mind awfully if she stayed just where she was until she felt better? She didn't feel too good at the moment, she really didn't.

Then hadn't she better lie down on the bed? Jack Noonan asked.

No, she said, she'd like to stay right where she was, in this chair. A little later perhaps, when she felt better, she would move.

So they left her there while they went about their business, searching the house. Occasionally one of the detectives asked her another question. Sometimes Jack Noonan spoke to her gently as he passed by. Her husband, he told her, had been killed by a blow on the back of the head administered with a heavy blunt instrument, almost certainly a large piece of metal. They were looking for the weapon. The murderer may have taken it with him, but on the other hand he may've thrown it away or hidden it somewhere on the premises.

'It's the old story,' he said. 'Get the weapon, and you've got the man.'

Later, one of the detectives came up and sat beside her. Did she know, he asked, of anything in the house that could've been used as the weapon? Would she mind having a look around to see if anything was missing – a very big spanner, for example, or a heavy metal vase.

They didn't have any heavy metal vases, she said.

'Or a big spanner?'

She didn't think they had a big spanner. But there might be some things like that in the garage.

The search went on. She knew that there were other policemen in the garden all around the house. She could hear their footsteps on the gravel outside, and sometimes she saw the flash of a torch through a chink in the curtains. It began to get late, nearly nine she noticed by the clock on the mantel. The four men searching the rooms seemed to be growing weary, a trifle exasperated.

'Jack,' she said, the next time Sergeant Noonan went by. 'Would you mind giving me a drink?'

'Sure I'll give you a drink. You mean this whisky?'

'Yes, please. But just a small one. It might make me feel better.'

He handed her the glass.

'Why don't you have one yourself,' she said. 'You must be awfully tired. Please do. You've been very good to me.'

'Well,' he answered. 'It's not strictly allowed, but I might take just a drop to keep me going.'

One by one the others came in and were persuaded to take a little nip of whisky. They stood around rather awkwardly with the drinks in their hands, uncomfortable in her presence, trying to say consoling things to her. Sergeant Noonan wandered into the kitchen, came out quickly and said, 'Look, Mrs Maloney. You know that oven of yours is still on, and the meat still inside.'

'Oh *dear* me!' she cried. 'So it is!'

'I better turn it off for you, hadn't I?'

'Will you do that, Jack. Thank you so much.'

When the sergeant returned the second time, she looked at him with her large, dark, tearful eyes. 'Jack Noonan,' she said.

'Yes?'

'Would you do me a small favour – you and these others?'

'We can try, Mrs Maloney.'

'Well,' she said. 'Here you all are, and good friends of dear Patrick's too, and helping to catch the man who killed him. You must be terrible hungry by now because it's long past your supper time, and I know Patrick would never forgive me, God bless his soul, if I allowed you to remain in his house without offering you decent hospitality. Why don't you eat up that lamb that's in the oven? It'll be cooked just right by now.'

'Wouldn't dream of it,' Sergeant Noonan said.

'Please,' she begged. 'Please eat it. Personally I couldn't touch a thing, certainly not what's been in the house when he was here. But it's all right for you. It'd be a favour to me if you'd eat it up. Then you can go on with your work again afterwards.'

There was a good deal of hesitating among the four policemen, but they were clearly hungry, and in the end they were persuaded to go into the kitchen and help themselves. The woman stayed where she was, listening to them through the open door, and she could hear them speaking among themselves, their voices thick and sloppy because their mouths were full of meat.

'Have some more, Charlie?'

'No. Better not finish it.'

'She *wants* us to finish it. She said so. Be doing her a favour.'

'Okay then. Give me some more.'

'That's the hell of a big club the guy must've used to hit poor Patrick,' one of them was saying. 'The doc says his skull was smashed all to pieces just like from a sledge-hammer.'

'That's why it ought to be easy to find.'

'Exactly what I say.'

'Whoever done it, they're not going to be carrying a thing like that around with them longer than they need.'

One of them belched.

37

'Personally, I think it's right here on the premises.'

'Probably right under our very noses. What you think Jack?'

And in the other room, Mary Maloney began to giggle.

Notes on The Landlady

In the previous story we witnessed the transformation of a happy suburban housewife into a murderess. Roald Dahl's characters often display bizarre or uncharacteristic behaviour. Often our initial perceptions of characters in these short stories are changed dramatically – there is always more to them than meets the eye. In 'The Landlady', Dahl alters our first impressions of the landlady through a series of subtle twists and turns.

What do you think?

The elements of horror within this story are not explicit – they are not described in gory detail. Although some of the ingredients of a horror story are set in place by Dahl, such as the uneasy atmosphere, the reader has to work out what is really happening by considering a number of subtle hints given at various stages of the action. While you are reading, think about:

- what the atmosphere is like at the start of the story
- the way Roald Dahl builds up feelings of tension and suspense
- what may have happened to the other guests at the boarding house.

Questions

Use relevant words and phrases from the story to support your answers to these questions:

1. What do we learn about Billy Weaver at the start of the story?
2. Is there anything to make the reader feel suspicious when Billy first arrives at the boarding house?
3. How might the landlady's comments about Billy's age and physical appearance be significant?
4. What clues does the writer give the reader that there may be something sinister about the boarding house?
5. What do you think happens to Billy Weaver at the end of the story?

Further activity

Imagine that after a long criminal investigation the landlady is found guilty of murdering Billy Weaver and her other guests. Write a newspaper report describing the events leading up to her conviction and the disturbing secrets uncovered at the boarding house.

The Landlady

Billy Weaver had travelled down from London on the slow afternoon train, with a change at Swindon on the way, and by the time he got to Bath it was about nine o'clock in the evening and the moon was coming up out of a clear starry sky over the houses opposite the station entrance. But the air was deadly cold and the wind was like a flat blade of ice on his cheeks.

'Excuse me,' he said, 'but is there a fairly cheap hotel not too far away from here?'

'Try The Bell and Dragon,' the porter answered, pointing down the road. 'They might take you in. It's about a quarter of a mile along on the other side.'

Billy thanked him and picked up his suitcase and set out to walk the quarter-mile to The Bell and Dragon. He had never been to Bath before. He didn't know anyone who lived there. But Mr Greenslade at the Head Office in London had told him it was a splendid city. 'Find your own lodgings,' he had said, 'and then go along and report to the Branch Manager as soon as you've got yourself settled.'

Billy was seventeen years old. He was wearing a new navy-blue overcoat, a new brown trilby hat, and a new brown suit, and he was feeling fine. He walked briskly down the street. He was trying to do everything briskly these days. Briskness, he had decided, was *the* one common characteristic of all successful businessmen. The big shots up at Head Office were absolutely fantastically brisk all the time. They were amazing.

There were no shops on this wide street that he was walking along, only a line of tall houses on each side, all of them identical. They had porches and pillars and four or five steps going up to their front doors, and it was obvious that once upon a time they had been very swanky residences. But now, even in the darkness, he could see that the paint was peeling from the woodwork on their doors and windows, and that the handsome white façades were cracked and blotchy from neglect.

Suddenly, in a downstairs window that was brilliantly illuminated by a street-lamp not six yards away, Billy caught sight of a printed notice propped up against the glass in one of the upper panes. It said BED AND BREAKFAST. There was a vase of pussy-willows, tall and beautiful, standing just underneath the notice.

He stopped walking. He moved a bit closer. Green curtains (some sort of velvety material) were hanging down on either side of the window. The pussy-willows looked wonderful beside them. He went right up and peered through the glass into the room, and the first thing he saw was a bright fire burning in the hearth. On the carpet in front of the fire, a pretty little dachshund was curled up asleep with its nose tucked into its belly. The room itself, so far as he could see in the half-darkness, was filled with pleasant furniture. There was a baby-grand piano and a big sofa and several plump armchairs; and in one corner he spotted a large parrot in a cage. Animals were usually a good sign in a place like this, Billy told himself; and all in all, it looked to him as though it would be a pretty decent house to stay in. Certainly it would be more comfortable than The Bell and Dragon.

On the other hand, a pub would be more congenial than a boarding-house. There would be beer and darts in the evenings, and lots of people to talk to, and it would probably be a good bit cheaper, too. He had stayed a couple of nights in a pub once before and he had liked it. He had never stayed in any boarding houses, and, to be perfectly honest, he was a tiny bit frightened of them. The name itself conjured up images of watery cabbage, rapacious landladies, and a powerful smell of kippers in the living-room.

After dithering about like this in the cold for two or three

42

minutes, Billy decided that he would walk on and take a look at The Bell and Dragon before making up his mind. He turned to go.

And now a queer thing happened to him. He was in the act of stepping back and turning away from the window when all at once his eye was caught and held in the most peculiar manner by the small notice that was there. BED AND BREAKFAST, it said. BED AND BREAKFAST, BED AND BREAKFAST, BED AND BREAKFAST.

Each word was like a large black eye staring at him through the glass, holding him, compelling him, forcing him to stay where he was and not to walk away from that house, and the next thing he knew, he was actually moving across from the window to the front door of the house, climbing the steps that led up to it, and reaching for the bell.

He pressed the bell. Far away in a back room he heard it ringing, and then *at once* – it must have been at once because he hadn't even had time to take his finger from the bell-button – the door swung open and a woman was standing there.

Normally you ring the bell and you have at least a half-minute's wait before the door opens. But this dame was like a jack-in-the-box. He pressed the bell – and out she popped! It made him jump.

She was about forty-five or fifty years old, and the moment she saw him, she gave him a warm welcoming smile.

'*Please* come in,' she said pleasantly. She stepped aside, holding the door wide open, and Billy found himself automatically starting forward into the house. The compulsion or, more accurately, the desire to follow after her into that house was extraordinarily strong.

'I saw the notice in the window,' he said, holding himself back.

'Yes, I know.'

'I was wondering about a room.'

43

'It's *all* ready for you, my dear,' she said. She had a round pink face and very gentle blue eyes.

'I was on my way to The Bell and Dragon,' Billy told her. 'But the notice in your window just happened to catch my eye.'

'My dear boy,' she said, 'why don't you come in out of the cold?'

'How much do you charge?'

'Five and sixpence a night, including breakfast.'

It was fantastically cheap. It was less than half of what he had been willing to pay.

'If that is too much,' she added, 'then perhaps I can reduce it just a tiny bit. Do you desire an egg for breakfast? Eggs are expensive at the moment. It would be sixpence less without the egg.'

'Five and sixpence is fine,' he answered. 'I should like very much to stay here.'

'I knew you would. Do come in.'

She seemed terribly nice. She looked exactly like the mother of one's best school-friend welcoming one into the house to stay for the Christmas holidays. Billy took off his hat, and stepped over the threshold.

'Just hang it there,' she said, 'and let me help you with your coat.'

There were no other hats or coats in the hall. There were no umbrellas, no walking-sticks – nothing.

'We have it *all* to ourselves,' she said, smiling at him over her shoulder as she led the way upstairs. 'You see, it isn't very often I have the pleasure of taking a visitor into my little nest.'

The old girl is slightly dotty, Billy told himself. But at five and sixpence a night, who gives a damn about that? 'I should've thought you'd be simply swamped with applicants,' he said politely.

'Oh, I am, my dear, I am, of course I am. But the trouble is that I'm inclined to be just a teeny weeny bit choosy and particular – if you see what I mean.'

'Ah, yes.'

'But I'm always ready. Everything is always ready day and night in this house just on the off-chance that an acceptable young gentleman will come along. And it is such a pleasure, my dear, such a very great pleasure when now and again I open the door and I see someone standing there who is just *exactly* right.' She was half-way up the stairs, and she paused with one hand on the stair-rail, turning her head and smiling down at him with pale lips. 'Like you,' she added, and her blue eyes travelled slowly all the way down the length of Billy's body, to his feet, and then up again.

On the first-floor landing she said to him, 'This floor is mine.'

They climbed up a second flight. 'And this one is *all* yours,' she said. 'Here's your room. I do hope you'll like it.' She took him into a small but charming front bedroom, switching on the light as she went in.

'The morning sun comes right in the window, Mr Perkins. It *is* Mr Perkins, isn't it?'

'No,' he said. 'It's Weaver.'

'Mr Weaver. How nice. I've put a water-bottle between the sheets to air them out, Mr Weaver. It's such a comfort to have a hot water-bottle in a strange bed with clean sheets, don't you agree? And you may light the gas fire at any time if you feel chilly.'

'Thank you,' Billy said. 'Thank you ever so much.' He noticed that the bedspread had been taken off the bed, and that the bedclothes had been neatly turned back on one side, all ready for someone to get in.

'I'm so glad you appeared,' she said, looking earnestly into his face. 'I was beginning to get worried.'

'That's all right,' Billy answered brightly. 'You mustn't worry about me.' He put his suitcase on the chair and started to open it.

'And what about supper, my dear? Did you manage to get anything to eat before you came here?'

'I'm not a bit hungry, thank you,' he said. 'I think I'll just go to bed as soon as possible because tomorrow I've got to get up rather early and report to the office.'

'Very well, then. I'll leave you now so that you can unpack. But before you go to bed, would you be kind enough to pop into the sitting-room on the ground floor and sign the book? Everyone has to do that because it's the law of the land, and we don't want to go breaking any laws at *this* stage in the proceedings, do we?' She gave him a little wave of the hand and went quickly out of the room and closed the door.

Now, the fact that his landlady appeared to be slightly off her rocker didn't worry Billy in the least. After all, she was not only harmless there was no question about that but she was also quite obviously a kind and generous soul. He guessed that she had probably lost a son in the war, or something like that, and had never got over it.

So a few minutes later, after unpacking his suitcase and washing his hands, he trotted downstairs to the ground floor and entered the living-room. His landlady wasn't there, but the fire was glowing in the hearth, and the little dachshund was still sleeping in front of it. The room was wonderfully warm and cosy. I'm a lucky fellow, he thought, rubbing his hands. This is a bit of all right.

He found the guest-book lying open on the piano, so he took out his pen and wrote down his name and address. There were only two other entries above his on the page, and, as one always does with guest-books, he started to read them. One was a Christopher Mulholland from Cardiff. The other was Gregory W. Temple from Bristol.

That's funny, he thought suddenly. Christopher Mulholland. It rings a bell.

Now where on earth had he heard that rather unusual name before?

Was he a boy at school? No. Was it one of his sister's numerous young men, perhaps, or a friend of his father's? No, no, it wasn't any of those. He glanced down again at the book.

| *Christopher Mulholland* | *231 Cathedral Road, Cardiff* |
| *Gregory W. Temple* | *27 Sycamore Drive, Bristol* |

As a matter of fact, now he came to think of it, he wasn't at all sure that the second name didn't have almost as much of a familiar ring about it as the first.

'Gregory Temple?' he said aloud, searching his memory. 'Christopher Mulholland …?'

'Such charming boys,' a voice behind him answered, and he turned and saw his landlady sailing into the room with a large silver tea-tray in her hands. She was holding it well out in front of her, and rather high up, as though the tray were a pair of reins on a frisky horse.

'They sound somehow familiar,' he said.

'They do? How interesting.'

'I'm almost positive I've heard those names before somewhere. Isn't that queer? Maybe it was in the newspapers. They weren't famous in any way, were they? I mean famous cricketers or footballers or something like that?'

'Famous,' she said, setting the tea-tray down on the low table in front of the sofa. 'Oh no, I don't think they were famous. But they were extraordinarily handsome, both of them, I can promise you that. They were tall and young and handsome, my dear, just exactly like you.'

Once more, Billy glanced down at the book. 'Look here,' he said, noticing the dates. 'This last entry is over two years old.'

'It is?'

'Yes, indeed. And Christopher Mulholland's is nearly a year before that – more than *three years* ago.'

'Dear me,' she said, shaking her head and heaving a dainty little sigh. 'I would never have thought it. How time does fly away from us all, doesn't it, Mr Wilkins?'

'It's Weaver,' Billy said. 'W-e-a-v-e-r.'

'Oh, of course it is?' she cried, sitting down on the sofa. 'How silly of me. I do apologise. In one ear and out the other, that's me, Mr Weaver.'

'You know something?' Billy said. 'Something that's really quite extraordinary about all this?'

'No, dear, I don't.'

'Well, you see – both of these names, Mulholland and Temple, I not only seem to remember each one of them separately, so to speak, but somehow or other, in some peculiar way, they both appear to be sort of connected together as well. As though they were both famous for the same sort of thing, if you see what I mean – like … well … like Dempsey and Tunney, for example, or Churchill and Roosevelt.'

'How amusing,' she said. 'But come over here now, dear, and sit down beside me on the sofa and I'll give you a nice cup of tea and a ginger biscuit before you go to bed.'

'You really shouldn't bother,' Billy said. 'I didn't mean you to do anything like that.' He stood by the piano, watching her as she fussed about with the cups and saucers. He noticed that she had small, white, quickly moving hands, and red fingernails.

'I'm almost positive it was in the newspapers I saw them,' Billy said. 'I'll think of it in a second. I'm sure I will.'

There is nothing more tantalising than a thing like this which lingers just outside the borders of one's memory. He hated to give up.

'Now wait a minute,' he said. 'Wait just a minute. Mulholland Christopher Mulholland … wasn't *that* the name of the Eton schoolboy who was on a walking-tour through the West Country, and then all of a sudden … '

'Milk?' she said. 'And sugar?'

'Yes, please. And then all of a sudden … '

'Eton schoolboy?' she said, 'Oh no, my dear, that can't possibly be right because *my* Mr Mulholland was certainly not an Eton schoolboy when he came to me. He was a Cambridge undergraduate. Come over here now and sit next to me and warm yourself in front of this lovely fire. Come on. Your tea's all ready for you.' She patted the empty place beside her on the sofa, and she sat there smiling at Billy and waiting for him to come over.

He crossed the room slowly, and sat down on the edge of the sofa. She placed his teacup on the table in front of him.

'*There* we are,' she said. 'How nice and cosy this is, isn't it?'

Billy started sipping his tea. She did the same. For half a minute or so, neither of them spoke. But Billy knew that she was looking at him. Her body was half-turned towards him and he could feel her eyes resting on his face, watching him over the rim of her teacup. Now and again, he caught a whiff of a peculiar smell that seemed to emanate directly from her person. It was not in the least unpleasant, and it reminded him well, he wasn't quite sure what it reminded him of. Pickled walnuts? New leather? Or was it the corridors of a hospital?

'Mr Mulholland was a great one for his tea,' she said at length. 'Never in my life have I seen anyone drink as much tea as dear, sweet Mr Mulholland.'

'I suppose he left fairly recently,' Billy said. He was still puzzling his head about the two names. He was positive now that he had seen them in the newspapers in the headlines.

'Left?' she said, arching her brows. 'But my dear boy, he never left. He's still here. Mr Temple is also here. They're on the third floor, both of them together.'

Billy set down his cup slowly on the table, and stared at his landlady. She smiled back at him, and then she put out one of her white hands and patted him comfortingly on the knee. 'How old are you, my dear?' she asked.

'Seventeen.'

'Seventeen!' she cried. 'Oh, it's the perfect age! Mr Mulholland was also seventeen. But I think he was a trifle shorter than you are, in fact I'm sure he was, and his teeth weren't *quite* so white. You have the most beautiful teeth, Mr Weaver, did you know that?'

'They're not as good as they look,' Billy said. 'They've got simply masses of fillings in them at the back.'

'Mr Temple, of course, was a little older,' she said, ignoring his remark. 'He was actually twenty-eight. And yet I never would have guessed it if he hadn't told me, never in my whole life. There wasn't a *blemish* on his body.'

'A what?' Billy said.

'His skin was *just* like a baby's.'

There was a pause. Billy picked up his teacup and took another sip of his tea, then he set it down again gently in its saucer. He waited for her to say something else, but she seemed to have lapsed into another of her silences. He sat there staring ahead of him into the far corner of the room, biting his lower lip.

'That parrot,' he said at last. 'You know something? It had me completely fooled when I first saw it through the window from the street. I could have sworn it was alive.'

'Alas, no longer.'

'It's most terribly clever the way it's been done,' he said. 'It doesn't look in the least bit dead. Who did it?'

'I did.'

'*You* did?'

'Of course,' she said. 'And have you met my little Basil as well?' She nodded towards the dachshund curled up so comfortably in front of the fire. Billy looked at it. And suddenly, he realized that this animal had all the time been just as silent and motionless as the parrot. He put out a hand and touched it gently on the top of its back. The back was hard and cold, and when he pushed the hair to one side with his fingers, he could see the skin underneath, greyish-black and dry and perfectly preserved.

'Good gracious me,' he said. 'How absolutely fascinating.' He turned away from the dog and stared with deep admiration at the little woman beside him on the sofa. 'It must be most awfully difficult to do a thing like that.'

'Not in the least,' she said. 'I stuff *all* my little pets myself when they pass away. Will you have another cup of tea?'

'No, thank you,' Billy said. The tea tasted faintly of bitter almonds, and he didn't much care for it.

'You did sign the book, didn't you?'

'Oh, yes.'

'That's good. Because later on, if I happen to forget what you were called, then I can always come down here and look it up. I still do that almost every day with Mr Mulholland and Mr ... Mr ... '

'Temple,' Billy said. 'Gregory Temple. Excuse my asking, but haven't there been *any* other guests here except them in the last two or three years?'

Holding her teacup high in one hand, inclining her head slightly to the left, she looked up at him out of the corners of her eyes and gave him another gentle little smile.

'No, my dear,' she said. 'Only you.'

Notes on The Champion of the World

Any illegal activity has an element of risk attached to it. To some people breaking the law may even involve excitement that comes from the danger of taking risks. In this story Roald Dahl writes about the unlawful pursuit of poaching as if it is an acceptable part of country life, involving many respected members of the local community.

What do you think?

The way in which Dahl describes poaching makes it appear exciting and appealing to the reader. In fact, he makes many aspects of the countryside appear delightful and interesting, and portrays a range of colourful characters. As you read the story, think about:

- how life in the countryside is made appealing
- what the writer thinks about poaching
- how the writer builds up tension and excitement
- your own attitude towards poaching after reading the story.

Questions

Support your answers to these questions with evidence and quotations from the text:

1. What evidence is there to suggest that Claud is nervous at the beginning of the story? Examine his actions and what he says.
2. How does the reader know that Claud loves poaching? Look at his behaviour and childhood recollections of his father.
3. What sort of person is Mr Victor Hazel? What do other characters in the story think of him?
4. Why is Claud 'white in the face' at the end of the story? What has gone wrong?

Further activity

Imagine you are Claud. Write a letter to a poaching friend describing how you poached 120 pheasants in one go. In your letter describe and explain:

- your attitude towards Victor Hazel and his gamekeepers
- what happens to you and the remaining pheasants in Bessie Organ's coal shed
- the implications for Victor Hazel's next shooting party.

The Champion of the World

All day, in between serving customers, we had been crouching over the table in the office of the filling-station, preparing the raisins. They were plump and soft and swollen from being soaked in water, and when you nicked them with a razor-blade the skin sprang open and the jelly stuff inside squeezed out as easily as you could wish.

But we had a hundred and ninety-six of them to do altogether and the evening was nearly upon us before we had finished.

'Don't they look marvellous!' Claud cried, rubbing his hands together hard. 'What time is it, Gordon?'

'Just after five.'

Through the window we could see a station-wagon pulling up at the pumps with a woman at the wheel and about eight children in the back eating ice-creams.

'We ought to be moving soon,' Claud said. 'The whole thing'll be a washout if we don't arrive before sunset, you realise that.' He was getting twitchy now. His face had the same flushed and pop-eyed look it got before a dog-race or when there was a date with Clarice in the evening.

We both went outside and Claud gave the woman the number of gallons she wanted. When she had gone, he remained standing in the middle of the driveway squinting anxiously up at the sun which was now only the width of a man's hand above the line of trees along the crest of the ridge on the far side of the valley.

'All right,' I said. 'Lock up.'

He went quickly from pump to pump, securing each nozzle in its holder with a small padlock.

'You'd better take off that yellow pullover,' he said.

'Why should I?'

'You'll be shining like a bloody beacon out there in the moonlight.'

'I'll be all right.'

'You will not,' he said. 'Take it off, Gordon, please. I'll see you in three minutes.' He disappeared into his caravan behind the filling-station, and I went indoors and changed my yellow pullover for a blue one.

When we met again outside, Claud was dressed in a pair of black trousers and a dark-green turtleneck sweater. On his head he wore a brown cloth cap with the peak pulled down low over his eyes, and he looked like an apache actor out of a nightclub.

'What's under there?' I asked, seeing the bulge at his waistline.

He pulled up his sweater and showed me two thin but very large white cotton sacks which were bound neat and tight around his belly. 'To carry the stuff,' he said darkly.

'I see.'

'Let's go,' he said.

'I still think we ought to take the car.'

'It's too risky. They'll see it parked.'

'But it's over three miles up to that wood.'

'Yes,' he said. 'And I suppose you realise we can get six months in the clink if they catch us.'

'You never told me that.'

'Didn't I?'

'I'm not coming,' I said. 'It's not worth it.'

'The walk will do you good, Gordon. Come on.'

It was a calm sunny evening with little wisps of brilliant white cloud hanging motionless in the sky, and the valley was cool and very quiet as the two of us began walking together along the grass verge on the side of the road that ran between the hills towards Oxford.

'You got the raisins?' Claud asked.

'They're in my pocket.'

'Good,' he said. 'Marvellous.'

Ten minutes later we turned left off the main road into a narrow lane with high hedges on either side and from now on it was all uphill.

'How many keepers are there?' I asked.

'Three.'

Claud threw away a half-finished cigarette. A minute later he lit another.

'I don't usually approve of new methods,' he said. 'Not on this sort of a job.'

'Of course.'

'But by God, Gordon, I think we're on to a hot one this time.'

'You do?'

'There's no question about it.'

'I hope you're right.'

'It'll be a milestone in the history of poaching,' he said. 'But don't you go telling a single soul how we've done it, you understand. Because if this ever leaked out we'd have every bloody fool in the district doing the same thing and there wouldn't be a pheasant left.'

'I won't say a word.'

'You ought to be very proud of yourself,' he went on. 'There's been men with brains studying this problem for hundreds of years and not one of them's ever come up with anything even a quarter as artful as you have. Why didn't you tell me about it before?'

'You never invited my opinion,' I said.

And that was the truth. In fact, up until the day before, Claud had never even offered to discuss with me the sacred subject of poaching. Often enough, on a summer's evening when work was finished, I had seen him with cap on head sliding quietly out of his caravan and disappearing up the road towards the woods; and sometimes, watching him through the windows of the filling-station, I would find myself wondering exactly what he was going to do, what wily tricks he was going to practise all alone up there under the trees in the dead of night. He seldom came back until very late, and never, absolutely never did he bring any of the spoils with him personally on his return. But the following afternoon – and I couldn't imagine how he did it – there would always be a pheasant or a hare or a brace of partridges hanging up in the shed behind the filling-station for us to eat.

This summer he had been particularly active, and during the last couple of months he had stepped up the tempo to a point where he was going out four and sometimes five nights a week. But that was not all. It seemed to me that recently his whole attitude towards poaching had undergone a subtle and mysterious change. He was more purposeful about it now, more tight-lipped and intense than before, and I had the impression that this was not so much a game any longer as a crusade, a sort of private war that Claud was waging single-handed against an invisible and hated enemy.

But who?

I wasn't sure about this, but I had a suspicion that it was none other than the famous Mr Victor Hazel himself, the owner of the land and the pheasants. Mr Hazel was a local brewer with an unbelievably arrogant manner. He was rich beyond words, and his property stretched for miles along either side of the valley. He was a self-made man with no charm at all and precious few virtues. He loathed all persons of humble station, having once been one of them himself, and he strove desperately to mingle with what he believed were the right kind of folk. He rode to hounds and gave shooting-parties and wore fancy waistcoats, and every weekday he drove an enormous black Rolls-Royce past the filling-station on his way to the brewery. As he flashed by, we would sometimes catch a glimpse of the great glistening brewer's face above the wheel, pink as a ham, all soft and inflamed from drinking too much beer.

Anyway, yesterday afternoon, right out of the blue, Claud had suddenly said to me, 'I'll be going on up to Hazel's woods again tonight. Why don't you come along?'

'Who, me?'

'It's about the last chance this year for pheasants,' he had said. 'The shooting-season opens Saturday and the birds'll be scattered all over the place after that – if there's any left.'

'Why the sudden invitation?' I had asked, greatly suspicious.

'No special reason, Gordon. No reason at all.'

'Is it risky?'

He hadn't answered this.

'I suppose you keep a gun or something hidden away up there?'

'A gun!' he cried, disgusted. 'Nobody ever *shoots* pheasants, didn't you know that? You've only got to fire a *cap-pistol* in Hazel's woods and the keepers'll be on you.'

'Then how do you do it?'

'Ah,' he said, and the eyelids drooped over the eyes, veiled and secretive.

There was a long pause. Then he said, 'Do you think you could keep your mouth shut if I was to tell you a thing or two?'

'Definitely.'

'I've never told this to anyone else in my whole life, Gordon.'

'I am greatly honoured,' I said. 'You can trust me completely.'

He turned his head, fixing me with pale eyes. The eyes were large and wet and ox-like, and they were so near to me that I could see my own face reflected upside down in the centre of each.

'I am now about to let you in on the three best ways in the world of poaching a pheasant,' he said. 'And seeing that you're the guest on this little trip, I am going to give you the choice of which one you'd like us to use tonight. How's that?'

'There's a catch in this.'

'There's no catch, Gordon. I swear it.'

57

'All right, go on.'

'Now, here's the thing,' he said. 'Here's the first big secret.' He paused and took a long suck at his cigarette. 'Pheasants,' he whispered softly, 'is *crazy* about raisins.'

'Raisins?'

'Just ordinary raisins. It's like a mania with them. My dad discovered that more than forty years ago just like he discovered all three of these methods I'm about to describe to you now.'

'I thought you said your dad was a drunk.'

'Maybe he was. But he was also a great poacher, Gordon. Possibly the greatest there's ever been in the history of England. My dad studied poaching like a scientist.'

'Is that so?'

'I mean it. I really mean it.'

'I believe you.'

'Do you know,' he said, 'my dad used to keep a whole flock of prime cockerels in the back yard purely for experimental purposes.'

'Cockerels?'

'That's right. And whenever he thought up some new stunt for catching a pheasant, he'd try it out on a cockerel first to see how it worked. That's how he discovered about raisins. It's also how he invented the horsehair method.'

Claud paused and glanced over his shoulder as though to make sure that there was nobody listening. 'Here's how it's done,' he said. 'First you take a few raisins and you soak them overnight in water to make them nice and plump and juicy. Then you get a bit of good stiff horsehair and you cut it up into half-inch lengths. Then you push one of these lengths of horsehair through the middle of each raisin so that there's about an eighth of an inch of it sticking out on either side. You follow?'

'Yes.'

'Now – the old pheasant comes along and eats one of these raisins. Right? And you're watching him from behind a tree. So what then?'

'I imagine it sticks in his throat.'

'That's obvious, Gordon. But here's the amazing thing. Here's what my dad discovered. The moment this happens, the bird *never moves his feet again*! He becomes absolutely rooted to the spot, and there he stands pumping his silly neck up and down just like it was a piston, and all you've got to do is walk calmly out from the place where you're hiding and pick him up in your hands.'

'I don't believe that.'

'I swear it,' he said. 'Once a pheasant's had the horsehair you can fire a rifle in his ear and he won't even jump. It's just one of those unexplainable little things. But it takes a genius to discover it.'

He paused, and there was a gleam of pride in his eye now as he dwelt for a moment or two upon the memory of his father, the great inventor.

'So that's Method Number One,' he said. 'Method Number Two is even more simple still. All you do is you have a fishing line. Then you bait the hook with a raisin and you fish for the pheasant just like you fish for a fish. You pay out the line about fifty yards and you lie there on your stomach in the bushes waiting till you get a bite. Then you haul him in.'

'I don't think your father invented that one.'

'It's very popular with fishermen,' he said, choosing not to hear me. 'Keen fishermen who can't get down to the seaside as often as they want. It gives them a bit of the old thrill. The only trouble is it's rather noisy. The pheasant squawks like hell as you haul him in, and then every keeper in the wood comes running.'

'What is Method Number Three?' I asked.

'Ah,' he said. 'Number Three's a real beauty. It was the last one my dad ever invented before he passed away.'

'His final great work?'

'Exactly, Gordon. And I can even remember the very day it happened, a Sunday morning it was, and suddenly my dad comes into the kitchen holding a huge white cockerel in his hands and he says, "I think I've got it!" There's a little smile on his face and a slime of glory in his eyes and he comes in very soft and quiet and he puts the bird down right in the middle of the kitchen table and he says, "By God, I think I've got a good one this time!" "A good what?" Mum says, looking up from the sink. "Horace, take that filthy bird off my table." The cockerel has a funny little paper hat over its head, like an ice-cream cone upside down, and my dad is pointing to it proudly. "Stroke him," he says. "He won't move an inch." The cockerel starts scratching away at the paper hat with one of its feet, but the hat seems to be stuck on with glue and it won't come off. "No bird in the world is going to run away once you cover up his eyes," my dad says, and he starts poking the cockerel with his finger and pushing it around on the table, but it doesn't take the slightest bit of notice. "You can have this one," he says, talking to Mum. "You can kill it and dish it up for dinner as a celebration of what I have just invented." And then straight away he takes me by the arm and marches me quickly out the door and off we go over the fields and up into the big forest the other side of Haddenham which used to belong to the Duke of Buckingham, and in less than two hours we get five lovely fat pheasants with no more trouble than it takes to go out and buy them in a shop.'

Claud paused for breath. His eyes were huge and moist and dreamy as they gazed back into the wonderful world of his youth.

'I don't quite follow this,' I said. 'How did he get the paper hats over the pheasants' heads up in the woods?'

'You'd never guess it.'

'I'm sure I wouldn't.'

'Then here it is. First of all you dig a little hole in the ground. Then you twist a piece of paper into the shape of a cone and you fit this into the hole, hollow end upward, like a cup. Then you smear the paper cup all around the inside with bird-lime and drop in a few raisins. At the same time you lay a trail of raisins along the ground leading up to it. Now – the old pheasant comes pecking along the trail, and when he gets to the hole he pops his head inside to gobble the raisins and the next thing he knows he's got a paper hat stuck over his eyes and he can't see a thing. Isn't it marvellous what some people think of, Gordon? Don't you agree?'

'Your dad was a genius,' I said.

'Then take your pick. Choose whichever one of the three methods you fancy and we'll use it tonight.'

'You don't think they're all just a trifle on the crude side, do you?'

'Crude!' he cried, aghast. 'Oh my God! And who's been having roasted pheasant in the house nearly every single day for the last six months and not a penny to pay?'

He turned and walked away towards the door of the workshop. I could see that he was deeply pained by my remark.

'Wait a minute,' I said. 'Don't go.'

'You want to come or don't you?'

'Yes, but let me ask you something first. I've just had a bit of an idea.'

'Keep it,' he said. 'You are talking about a subject you don't know the first thing about.'

'Do you remember that bottle of sleeping-pills the doc gave me last month when I had a bad back?'

'What about them?'

'Is there any reason why those wouldn't work on a pheasant?'

Claud closed his eyes and shook his head pityingly from side to side.

'Wait,' I said.

'It's not worth discussing,' he said. 'No pheasant in the world is going to swallow those lousy red capsules. Don't you know any better than that?'

'You are forgetting the raisins,' I said. 'Now listen to this. We take a raisin. Then we soak it till it swells. Then we make a tiny slit in one side of it with a razor-blade. Then we hollow it out a little. Then we open up one of my red capsules and pour all the powder into the raisin. Then we get a needle and cotton and very carefully we sew up the slit. Now … '

Out of the corner of my eye, I saw Claud's mouth slowly beginning to open.

'Now,' I said. 'We have a nice clean-looking raisin with two and a half grains of seconal inside it, and let me tell *you* something now. That's enough dope to knock the average *man* unconscious, never mind about *birds*!'

I paused for ten seconds to allow the full impact of this to strike home.

'What's more, with this method we could operate on a really grand scale. We could prepare *twenty* raisins if we felt like it, and all we'd have to do is scatter them around the feeding grounds at sunset and then walk away. Half an hour later we'd come back, and the pills would be beginning to work, and the pheasants would be up in the trees by then, roosting, and they'd be starting to feel groggy, and they'd be wobbling and trying to keep their balance, and soon every pheasant that had eaten *one single raisin* would keel over unconscious and fall to the ground. My dear boy, they'd be dropping out of the trees like apples, and all we'd have to do is walk around picking them up!'

Claud was staring at me, rapt.

'Oh Christ,' he said softly.

'And they'd never catch us either. We'd simply stroll through the woods dropping a few raisins here and there as we went and even if they were *watching* us they wouldn't notice anything.'

'Gordon,' he said, laying a hand on my knee and gazing at me with eyes large and bright as two stars. 'If this thing works, it will *revolutionise* poaching.'

'I'm glad to hear it.'

'How many pills have you got left?' he asked.

'Forty-nine. There were fifty in the bottle and I've only used one.'

'Forty-nine's not enough. We want at least two hundred.'

'Are you mad!' I cried.

He walked slowly away and stood by the door with his back to me, gazing at the sky.

'Two hundred's the bare minimum,' he said quietly. 'There's really not much point in doing it unless we have two hundred.'

What is it now, I wondered. What the hell's he trying to do?

'This is the last chance we'll have before the season opens,' he said.

'I couldn't possibly get any more.'

'You wouldn't want us to come back empty-handed, would you?'

'But why so *many*?'

Claud turned his head and looked at me with large innocent eyes. 'Why not?' he said gently. 'Do you have any objection?'

My God, I thought suddenly. The crazy bastard is out to wreck Mr Victor Hazel's opening-day shooting-party.

'You get us two hundred of those pills,' he said, 'and then it'll be worth doing.'

'I can't.'

'You could try, couldn't you?'

Mr Hazel's party took place on the first of October every year and it was a very famous event. Debilitated gentlemen in

63

tweed suits, some with titles and some who were merely rich, motored in from miles around with their gun-bearers and dogs and wives, and all day long the noise of shooting rolled across the valley. There were always enough pheasants to go round, for each summer the woods were methodically restocked with dozens and dozens of young birds at incredible expense. I had heard it said that the cost of rearing and keeping each pheasant up to the time when it was ready to be shot was well over five pounds (which is approximately the price of two hundred loaves of bread). But to Mr Hazel it was worth every penny of it. He became, if only for a few hours, a big cheese in a little world and even the Lord Lieutenant of the County slapped him on the back and tried to remember his first name when he said good-bye.

'How would it be if we just reduced the dose?' Claud asked. 'Why couldn't we divide the contents of one capsule among four raisins?'

'I suppose you could if you wanted to.'

'But would a quarter of a capsule be strong enough for each bird?'

One simply had to admire the man's nerve. It was dangerous enough to poach a single pheasant up in those woods at this time of year and here he was planning to knock off the bloody lot.

'A quarter would be plenty,' I said.

'You're sure of that?'

'Work it out for yourself. It's all done by bodyweight. You'd still be giving about twenty times more than is necessary.'

'Then we'll quarter the dose,' he said, rubbing his hands. He paused and calculated for a moment. 'We'll have one hundred and ninety-six raisins!'

'Do you realise what that involves?' I said. 'They'll take hours to prepare.'

'What of it!' he cried. 'We'll go tomorrow instead. We'll soak the raisins overnight and then we'll have all morning and afternoon to get them ready.'

And that was precisely what we did.

Now, twenty-four hours later, we were on our way. We had been walking steadily for about forty minutes and we were nearing the point where the lane curved round to the right and ran along the crest of the hill towards the big wood where the pheasants lived. There was about a mile to go.

'I don't suppose by any chance these keepers might be carrying guns?' I asked.

'All keepers carry guns,' Claud said. I had been afraid of that.

'It's for the vermin mostly.'

'Ah.'

'Of course there's no guarantee they won't take a pot at a poacher now and again.'

'You're joking.'

'Not at all. But they only do it from behind. Only when you're running away. They like to pepper you in the legs at about fifty yards.'

'They can't do that!' I cried. 'It's a criminal offence!'

'So is poaching,' Claud said.

We walked on awhile in silence. The sun was below the high hedge on our right now and the lane was in shadow.

'You can consider yourself lucky this isn't thirty years ago,' he went on. 'They used to shoot you on sight in those days.'

'Do you believe that?'

'I know it,' he said. 'Many's the night when I was a nipper I've gone into the kitchen and seen my old dad lying face downward on the table and Mum standing over him digging the grapeshot out of his buttocks with a potato knife.'

'Stop,' I said. 'It makes me nervous.'

'You believe me, don't you?'

'Yes, I believe you.'

'Towards the end he was so covered in tiny little white scars he looked exactly like it was snowing.'

'Yes,' I said. 'All right.'

'Poacher's arse, they used to call it,' Claud said. 'And there wasn't a man in the whole village who didn't have a bit of it one way or another. But my dad was the champion.'

'Good luck to him,' I said.

'I wish to hell he was here now,' Claud said, wistful. 'He'd have given anything in the world to be coming with us on this job tonight.'

'He could take my place,' I said. 'Gladly.'

We had reached the crest of the hill and now we could see the wood ahead of us, huge and dark with the sun going down behind the trees and little sparks of gold shining through.

'You'd better let me have those raisins,' Claud said. I gave him the bag and he slid it gently into his trouser pocket.

'No talking once we're inside,' he said. 'Just follow me and try not to go snapping any branches.'

Five minutes later we were there. The lane ran right up to the wood itself and then skirted the edge of it for about three hundred yards with only a little hedge between. Claud slipped through the hedge on all fours and I followed.

It was cool and dark inside the wood. No sunlight came in at all.

'This is spooky,' I said.

'Ssshh!'

Claud was very tense. He was walking just ahead of me, picking his feet up high and putting them down gently on the moist ground. He kept his head moving all the time, the eyes sweeping slowly from side to side, searching for danger. I tried doing the same, but soon I began to see a keeper behind every tree, so I gave it up.

Then a large patch of sky appeared ahead of us in the roof of the forest and I knew that this must be the clearing. Claud had told me that the clearing was the place where the young birds were introduced into the woods in early July, where they were fed and watered and guarded by the keepers, and where many of them stayed from force of habit until the shooting began.

'There's always plenty of pheasants in the clearing,' he had said.

'Keepers too, I suppose.'

'Yes, but there's thick bushes all around and that helps.'

We were now advancing in a series of quick crouching spurts, running from tree to tree and stopping and waiting and listening and running on again, and then at last we were kneeling safely behind a big clump of alder right on the edge of the clearing and Claud was grinning and nudging me in the ribs and pointing through the branches at the pheasants.

The place was absolutely stiff with birds. There must have been two hundred of them at least strutting around among the tree-stumps.

'You see what I mean?' Claud whispered.

It was an astonishing sight, a sort of poacher's dream come true. And how close they were! Some of them were not more than ten paces from where we knelt. The hens were plump and creamy-brown and they were so fat their breast-feathers almost brushed the ground as they walked. The cocks were slim and beautiful, with long tails and brilliant red patches around the eyes, like scarlet spectacles. I glanced at Claud. His big ox-like face was transfixed in ecstasy. The mouth was slightly open and the eyes had a kind of glazy look about them as they stared at the pheasants.

I believe that all poachers react in roughly the same way as this on sighting game. They are like women who sight large emeralds in a jeweller's window, the only difference being that the women are less dignified in the methods they employ later on to acquire the loot. Poacher's arse is nothing to the punishment that a female is willing to endure.

'Ah-ha,' Claud said softly. 'You see the keeper?'

'Where?'

'Over the other side, by that big tree. Look carefully.'

'My God!'

'It's all right. He can't see *us*.'

We crouched close to the ground, watching the keeper. He was a smallish man with a cap on his head and a gun under his arm. He never moved. He was like a little post standing there.

'Let's go,' I whispered.

The keeper's face was shadowed by the peak of his cap, but it seemed to me that he was looking directly at us.

'I'm not staying here,' I said.

'Hush,' Claud said.

Slowly, never taking his eyes from the keeper, he reached into his pocket and brought out a single raisin. He placed it in the palm of his right hand, and then quickly, with a little flick of the wrist, he threw the raisin high into the air. I watched it as it went sailing over the bushes and I saw it land within a yard or so of two hen birds standing together beside an old tree-stump. Both birds turned their heads sharply at the drop of the raisin. Then one of them hopped over and made a quick peck at the ground and that must have been it.

I glanced up at the keeper. He hadn't moved.

Claud threw a second raisin into the clearing; then a third, and a fourth, and a fifth.

At this point, I saw the keeper turn away his head in order to survey the wood behind him.

Quick as a flash, Claud pulled the paper bag out of his pocket and tipped a huge pile of raisins into the cup of his right hand.

'Stop,' I said.

But with a great sweep of the arm he flung the whole handful high over the bushes into the clearing.

They fell with a soft little patter, like raindrops on dry leaves, and every single pheasant in the place must either have seen them coming or heard them fall. There was a flurry of wings and a rush to find the treasure.

The keeper's head flicked round as though there were a spring inside his neck. The birds were all pecking away madly at the raisins. The keeper took two quick paces forward and for a moment I thought he was going in to investigate. But then he stopped, and his face came up and his eyes began travelling slowly around the perimeter of the clearing.

'Follow me,' Claud whispered. 'And *keep down.*' He started crawling away swiftly on all fours, like some kind of a monkey.

I went after him. He had his nose close to the ground and his huge tight buttocks were winking at the sky and it was easy to see now how poacher's arse had come to be an occupational disease among the fraternity.

We went along like this for about a hundred yards.

'Now run,' Claud said.

We got to our feet and ran, and a few minutes later we emerged through the hedge into the lovely open safety of the lane.

'It went marvellous,' Claud said, breathing heavily. 'Didn't it go absolutely marvellous?' The big face was scarlet and glowing with triumph.

'It was a mess,' I said.

'What!' he cried.

'Of course it was. We can't possibly go back now. That keeper knows there was someone there.'

'He knows nothing,' Claud said. 'In another five minutes it'll be pitch dark inside the wood and he'll be sloping off home to his supper.'

'I think I'll join him.'

'You're a great poacher,' Claud said. He sat down on the grassy bank under the hedge and lit a cigarette.

The sun had set now and the sky was a pale smoke blue, faintly glazed with yellow. In the woods behind us the shadows and the spaces in between the trees were turning from grey to black.

'How long does a sleeping-pill take to work?' Claud asked.

'Look out,' I said, 'There's someone coming.'

The man had appeared suddenly and silently out of the dusk and he was only thirty yards away when I saw him.

'Another bloody keeper,' Claud said.

We both looked at the keeper as he came down the lane towards us. He had a shotgun under his arm and there was a black Labrador walking at his heels. He stopped when he was a few paces away and the dog stopped with him and stayed behind him, watching us through the keeper's legs.

'Good evening,' Claud said, nice and friendly.

This one was a tall bony man about forty with a swift eye and a hard cheek and hard dangerous hands.

'I know you,' he said softly, coming closer. 'I know the both of you.'

Claud didn't answer this.

'You're from the fillin'-station. Right?'

His lips were thin and dry, with some sort of a brownish crust over them.

'You're Cubbage and Hawes and you're from the fillin'-station on the main road, Right?'

'What are we playing?' Claud said. 'Twenty Questions?' The keeper spat out a big gob of spit and I saw it go floating through the air and land with a plop on a patch of dry dust six inches from Claud's feet. It looked like a little baby oyster lying there.

'Beat it,' the man said. 'Go on. Get out.'

Claud sat on the bank smoking his cigarette and looking at the gob of spit.

'Go on,' the man said. 'Get out.'

When he spoke, the upper lip lifted above the gum and I could see a row of small discoloured teeth, one of them black, the others quince and ochre.

'This happens to be a public highway,' Claud said. 'Kindly do not molest us.'

The keeper shifted the gun from his left arm to his right.

'You're loiterin',' he said, 'with intent to commit a felony. I could run you in for that.'

'No you couldn't,' Claud said. All this made me rather nervous.

'I've had my eye on you for some time,' the keeper said, looking at Claud.

'It's getting late,' I said. 'Shall we stroll on?'

Claud flipped away his cigarette and got slowly to his feet.

'All right,' he said. 'Let's go.'

We wandered off down the lane the way we had come, leaving the keeper standing there, and soon the man was out of sight in the half-darkness behind us.

'That's the head keeper,' Claud said. 'His name is Rabbetts.'

'Let's get the hell out,' I said.

'Come in here,' Claud said.

There was a gate on our left leading into a field and we climbed over it and sat down behind the hedge.

'Mr Rabbetts is also due for his supper,' Claud said. 'You mustn't worry about him.'

We sat quietly behind the hedge waiting for the keeper to walk past us on his way home. A few stars were showing and a bright three-quarter moon was coming up over the hills behind us in the cast.

'Here he is,' Claud whispered. 'Don't move.'

The keeper came loping softly up the lane with the dog padding quick and soft-footed at his heels, and we watched them through the hedge as they went by.

'He won't be coming back tonight,' Claud said.

'How do you know that?'

'A keeper never waits for you in the wood if he knows where you live. He goes to your house and hides outside and watches for you to come back.'

'That's worse.'

'No, it isn't, not if you dump the loot somewhere else before you go home. He can't touch you then.'

'What about the other one, the one in the clearing?'

'He's gone too.'

'You can't be sure of that.'

'I've been studying these bastards for months, Gordon, honest I have. I know all their habits. There's no danger.'

Reluctantly I followed him back into the wood. It was pitch dark in there now and very silent, and as we moved cautiously forward the noise of our footsteps seemed to go echoing around the walls of the forest as though we were walking in a cathedral.

'Here's where we threw the raisins,' Claud said. I peered through the bushes.

The clearing lay dim and milky in the moonlight.

'You're quite sure the keeper's gone?'

'I *know* he's gone.'

I could just see Claud's face under the peak of his cap, the pale lips, the soft pale cheeks, and the large eyes with a little spark of excitement dancing slowly in each.

'Are they roosting?'

'Yes.'

'Whereabouts?'

'All around. They don't go far.'

'What do we do next?'

'We stay here and wait. I brought you a light,' he added, and he handed me one of those small pocket flashlights shaped like a fountain-pen. 'You may need it.'

I was beginning to feel better. 'Shall we see if we can spot some of them sitting in the trees?' I said.

'No.'

'I should like to see how they look when they're roosting.'

'This isn't a nature-study.' Claud said. 'Please be quiet.'

We stood there for a long time waiting for something to happen.

'I've just had a nasty thought.' I said. 'If a bird can keep its balance on a branch when it's asleep, then surely there isn't any reason why the pills should make it fall down.'

Claud looked at me quick.

'After all,' I said, 'it's not dead. It's still only sleeping.'

'It's doped,' Claud said.

'But that's just a *deeper* sort of sleep. Why should we expect it to fall down just because it's in a *deeper* sleep?'

There was a gloomy silence.

'We should've tried it with chickens,' Claud said. 'My dad would've done that.'

'Your dad was a genius,' I said.

At that moment there came a soft thump from the wood behind us.

'Hey!'

'Ssshh!'

We stood listening.

Thump.

'There's another!'

It was a deep muffled sound as though a bag of sand had been dropped from about shoulder height.

Thump!

'They're pheasants!' I cried.

'Wait!'

'I'm sure they're pheasants!'

Thump! Thump!

'You're right!'

We ran back into the wood.

'Where were they?'

'Over here! Two of them were over here!'

73

'I thought they were this way.'

'Keep looking!' Claud shouted. 'They can't be far.' We searched for about a minute.

'Here's one!' he called.

When I got to him he was holding a magnificent cock-bird in both hands. We examined it closely with our flashlights.

'It's doped to the gills,' Claud said. 'It's still alive, I can feel its heart, but it's doped to the bloody gills.'

Thump!

'There's another!'

Thump! Thump!

'Two more!'

Thump!

Thump! Thump! Thump!

'Jesus Christ!'

Thump! Thump! Thump! Thump!

Thump! Thump!

All around us the pheasants were starting to rain down out of the trees. We began rushing around madly in the dark, sweeping the ground with our flashlights.

Thump! Thump! Thump! This lot fell almost on top of me. I was right under the tree as they came down and I found all three of them immediately – two cocks and a hen. They were limp and warm, the feathers wonderfully soft in the hand.

'Where shall I put them?' I called out. I was holding them by the legs.

'Lay them here, Gordon! Just pile them up here where it's light.'

Claud was standing on the edge of the clearing with the moonlight streaming down all over him and a great bunch of pheasants in each hand. His face was bright, his eyes big and bright and wonderful, and he was staring around him like a child who has just discovered that the whole world is made of chocolate.

Thump!

Thump! Thump!

'I don't like it,' I said. 'It's too many.'

'It's beautiful!' he cried and he dumped the birds he was carrying and ran off to look for more.

Thump! Thump! Thump! Thump!

Thump!

It was easy to find them now. There were one or two lying under every tree. I quickly collected six more, three in each hand, and ran back and dumped them with the others. Then six more. Then six more after that.

And still they kept falling.

Claud was in a whirl of ecstasy now, dashing about like a mad ghost under the trees. I could see the beam of his flashlight waving around in the dark and each time he found a bird he gave a little yelp of triumph.

Thump! Thump! Thump!

'That bugger Hazel ought to hear this!' he called out.

'Don't shout,' I said. 'It frightens me.'

'What's that?'

'Don't *shout*. There might be keepers.'

'Screw the keepers!' he cried. 'They're all eating!'

For three or four minutes, the pheasants kept on falling. Then suddenly they stopped.

'Keep searching!' Claud shouted. 'There's plenty more on the ground!'

'Don't you think we ought to get out while the going's good?'

'No,' he said.

We went on searching. Between us we looked under every tree within a hundred yards of the clearing, north, south, east, and west, and I think we found most of them in the end. At the collecting-point there was a pile of pheasants as big as a bonfire.

'It's a miracle,' Claud was saying. 'It's a bloody miracle.' He was staring at them in a kind of trance.

'We'd better just take half a dozen each and get out quick,' I said.

'I would like to count them, Gordon.'

'There's no time for that.'

'I must count them.'

'No,' I said. 'Come on.'

'One …

'Two …

'Three …

'Four … '

He began counting them very carefully, picking up each bird in turn and laying it carefully to one side. The moon was directly overhead now and the whole clearing was brilliantly illuminated.

'I'm not standing around here like this,' I said. I walked back a few paces and hid myself in the shadows, waiting for him to finish.

'A hundred and seventeen … a hundred and eighteen … a hundred and nineteen … *a hundred and twenty*!' he cried. '*One hundred and twenty birds*! It's an all-time record!'

I didn't doubt it for a moment.

'The most my dad ever got in one night was fifteen and he was drunk for a week afterwards!'

'You're the champion of the world,' I said. 'Are you ready now?'

'One minute,' he answered and he pulled up his sweater and proceeded to unwind the two big white cotton sacks from around his belly. 'Here's yours,' he said, handing one of them to me. 'Fill it up quick.'

The light of the moon was so strong I could read the small print along the base of the sack. J.W. CRUMP, it said. KESTON FLOUR MILLS, LONDON SW 17.

'You don't think that bastard with the brown teeth is watching us this very moment from behind a tree?'

'There's no chance of that,' Claud said. 'He's down at the filling-station like I told you, waiting for us to come home.'

We started loading the pheasants into the sacks. They were soft and floppy-necked and the skin underneath the feathers was still warm.

'There'll be a taxi waiting for us in the lane,' Claud said.

'What?'

'I always go back in a taxi, Gordon, didn't you know that?' I told him I didn't.

'A taxi is anonymous,' Claud said. 'Nobody knows who's inside a taxi except the driver. My dad taught me that.'

'Which driver?'

'Charlie Kinch. He's only too glad to oblige.'

We finished loading the pheasants, and I tried to hump my bulging sack on to my shoulder. My sack had about sixty birds inside it, and it must have weighed a hundredweight and a half, at least. 'I can't carry this,' I said. 'We'll have to leave some of them behind.'

'Drag it,' Claud said. 'Just pull it behind you.'

We started off through the pitch-black woods, pulling the pheasants behind us. 'We'll never make it all the way back to the village like this,' I said.

'Charlie's never let me down yet,' Claud said.

We came to the margin of the wood and peered through the hedge into the lane. Claud said, 'Charlie boy' very softly and the old man behind the wheel of the taxi not five yards away poked his head out into the moonlight and gave us a sly toothless grin. We slid through the hedge, dragging the sacks after us along the ground.

'Hullo!' Charlie said. 'What's this?'

'It's cabbages,' Claud told him. 'Open the door.'

Two minutes later we were safely inside the taxi, cruising slowly down the hill towards the village.

It was all over now bar the shouting. Claud was triumphant, bursting with pride and excitement, and he kept leaning forward and tapping Charlie Kinch on the shoulder and saying, 'How about it, Charlie? How about this for a haul?' and Charlie kept glancing back popeyed at the huge bulging sacks lying on the floor between us and saying, 'Jesus Christ, man, how did you do it?'

'There's six brace of them for you, Charlie,' Claud said. And Charlie said, 'I reckon pheasants is going to be a bit scarce up at Mr Victor Hazel's opening-day shoot this year,' and Claud said, 'I imagine they are, Charlie, I imagine they are.'

'What in God's name are you going to do with a hundred and twenty pheasants?' I asked.

'Put them in cold storage for the winter,' Claud said. 'Put them in with the dogmeat in the deep-freeze at the filling-station.'

'Not tonight, I trust?'

'No, Gordon, not tonight. We leave them at Bessie's house tonight.'

'Bessie who?'

'Bessie Organ.'

'Bessie *Organ*!'

'Bessie always delivers my game, didn't you know that?'

'I don't know anything,' I said. I was completely stunned. Mrs Organ was the wife of the Reverend Jack Organ, the local vicar.

'Always choose a respectable woman to deliver your game,' Claud announced. 'That's correct, Charlie, isn't it?'

'Bessie's a right smart girl,' Charlie said.

We were driving through the village now and the street-lamps were still on and the men were wandering home from the pubs. I saw Will Prattley letting himself in quietly by the side-door of his fishmonger's shop and Mrs Prattley's head was sticking out of the window just above him, but he didn't know it.

78

'The vicar is very partial to roasted pheasant,' Claud said.

'He hangs it eighteen days,' Charlie said, 'then he gives it a couple of good shakes and all the feathers drop off.'

The taxi turned left and swung in through the gates of the vicarage. There were no lights on in the house and nobody met us. Claud and I dumped the pheasants in the coal shed at the rear, and then we said good-bye to Charlie Kinch and walked back in the moonlight to the filling-station, empty-handed. Whether or not Mr Rabbetts was watching us as we went in, I do not know. We saw no sign of him.

'Here she comes,' Claud said to me the next morning.

'Who?'

'Bessie – Bessie Organ.' He spoke the name proudly and with a slight proprietary air, as though he were a general referring to his bravest officer.

I followed him outside.

'Down there,' he said, pointing.

Far away down the road I could see a small female figure advancing towards us.

'What's she pushing?' I asked.

Claud gave me a sly look.

'There's only one safe way of delivering game,' he announced, 'and that's under a baby.'

'Yes,' I murmured, 'yes, of course.'

'That'll he young Christopher Organ in there, aged one and a half. He's a lovely child, Gordon.'

I could just make out the small dot of a baby sitting high up in the pram, which had its hood folded down.

'There's sixty or seventy pheasants at least under that little nipper,' Claud said happily. 'You just imagine that.'

'You can't put sixty or seventy pheasants in a pram.'

'You can if it's got a good deep well underneath it, and if you take out the mattress and pack them in tight, right up to the top.

79

All you need then is a sheet. You'll be surprised how little room a pheasant takes up when it's limp.'

We stood beside the pumps waiting for Bessie Organ to arrive. It was one of those warm windless September mornings with a darkening sky and a smell of thunder in the air.

'Right through the village bold as brass,' Claud said. 'Good old Bessie.'

'She seems in rather a hurry to me.'

Claud lit a new cigarette from the stub of the old one. 'Bessie is never in a hurry,' he said.

'She certainly isn't walking normal,' I told him. 'You look.' He squinted at her through the smoke of his cigarette. Then he took the cigarette out of his mouth and looked again.

'Well?' I said.

'She does seem to be going a tiny bit quick, doesn't she?' he said carefully.

'She's going damn quick.'

There was a pause. Claud was beginning to stare very hard at the approaching woman.

'Perhaps she doesn't want to be caught in the rain, Gordon. I'll bet that's exactly what it is, she thinks it's going to rain and she don't want the baby to get wet.'

'Why doesn't she put the hood up?' He didn't answer this.

'She's *running*!' I cried. 'Look!' Bessie had suddenly broken into a full sprint.

Claud stood very still, watching the woman; and in the silence that followed I fancied I could hear a baby screaming.

'What's up?'

He didn't answer.

'There's something wrong with that baby,' I said. 'Listen.' At this point, Bessie was about two hundred yards away from us but closing fast.

'Can you hear him now?' I said.

'Yes.'

'He's yelling his head off.'

The small shrill voice in the distance was growing louder every second, frantic, piercing, nonstop, almost hysterical.

'He's having a fit,' Claud announced.

'I think he must be.'

'That's why she's running, Gordon. She wants to get him in here quick and put him under a cold tap.'

'I'm sure you're right,' I said. 'In fact I know you're right. Just listen to that noise.'

'If it isn't a fit, you can bet your life it's something like it.'

'I quite agree.'

Claud shifted his feet uneasily on the gravel of the driveway. 'There's a thousand and one different things keep happening every day to little babies like that,' he said.

'Of course.'

'I knew a baby once who caught his fingers in the spokes of the pram wheel. He lost the lot. It cut them clean off.'

'Yes.'

'Whatever it is,' Claud said, 'I wish to Christ she'd stop running.'

A long truck loaded with bricks came up behind Bessie and the driver slowed down and poked his bead out the window to stare. Bessie ignored him and flew on, and she was so close now I could see her big red face with the mouth wide open, panting for breath. I noticed she was wearing white gloves on her hands, very prim and dainty, and there was a funny little white hat to match perched right on the top of her head, like a mushroom.

Suddenly, out of the pram, straight up into the air, flew an enormous pheasant!

Claud let out a cry of horror.

The fool in the truck going along beside Bessie started roaring with laughter.

The pheasant flapped around drunkenly for a few seconds, then it lost height and landed in the grass by the side of the road.

A grocer's van came up behind the truck and began hooting to get by. Bessie kept running.

Then – *whoosh!* – a second pheasant flew up out of the pram. Then a third, and a fourth. Then a fifth.

'My God!' I said. 'It's the pills! They're wearing off!'

Claud didn't say anything.

Bessie covered the last fifty yards at a tremendous pace, and she came swinging into the driveway of the filling-station with birds flying up out of the pram in all directions.

'What the hell's going on?' she cried.

'Go round the back!' I shouted. 'Go round the back!' But she pulled up sharp against the first pump in the line, and before we could reach her she had seized the screaming infant in her arms and dragged him clear.

'No! No!' Claud cried, racing towards her. 'Don't lift the baby! Put him back! Hold down the sheet!' But she wasn't even listening, and with the weight of the child suddenly lifted away, a great cloud of pheasants rose up out of the pram, fifty or sixty of them, at least, and the whole sky above us was filled with huge brown birds flapping their wings furiously to gain height.

Claud and I started running up and down the driveway waving our arms to frighten them off the premises. 'Go away!' we shouted. 'Shoo! Go away!' But they were too dopey still to take any notice of us and within half a minute down they came again and settled themselves like a swarm of locusts all over the front of my filling-station. The place was covered with them. They sat wing to wing along the edges of the roof and on the concrete canopy that came out over the pumps, and a dozen at least were clinging to the sill of the office window. Some had flown down on to the rack that held the bottles of lubricating-oil, and others were sliding about on the bonnets of my second-hand cars. One cockbird with a fine tail was perched superbly on top of a petrol pump, and quite a number, those that were too drunk to stay aloft, simply squatted in the driveway at our feet, fluffing their feathers and blinking their small eyes.

Across the road, a line of cars had already started forming behind the brick-lorry and the grocery-van, and people were opening their doors and getting out and beginning to cross over to have a closer look. I glanced at my watch. It was twenty to nine. Any moment now, I thought, a large black car is going to come streaking along the road from the direction of the village, and the car will be a Rolls, and the face behind the wheel will he the great glistening brewer's face of Mr Victor Hazel.

'They near pecked him to pieces!' Bessie was shouting, clasping the screaming baby to her bosom.

'You go on home, Bessie,' Claud said, white in the face.

'Lock up,' I said. 'Put out the sign. We've gone for the day.'

Notes on Galloping Foxley

Routine is a big part of life. Most people are creatures of habit and go to school or work, visiting the same places and seeing the same people time and time again. In this story an elderly commuter experiences unwelcome disruption to his routine and predictable life in the form of an unpleasant acquaintance from his past life. The experience stirs up memories of cruelty and suffering. Very often it is unpleasant memories which are the hardest to forget.

What do you think?

By recalling memories of Perkins' childhood, Roald Dahl is able to write about some of his own cruel experiences at his old school. The harsh and disciplined environment of the public school system, with its strict rules and routines, left an impression on its pupils that lived on with them throughout their lives. As you read, think about:

- how William Perkins' experiences at school may have contributed to his ideas and behaviour as an adult
- why he remembers his encounters with Galloping Foxley so clearly.

Questions

Look for passages in the text which provide evidence to support your answers to these questions:

1. Why does the narrator, William Perkins, enjoy commuting to work by train?

2. What sort of man is William Perkins? How has our understanding of him changed by the end of the story?

3. What does Perkins dislike about the stranger's appearance and behaviour? What does he mean by 'he was not one of us'?

4. What do you consider to be the worst thing that Galloping Foxley did to William Perkins at school?

5. Describe how the narrator intends to get his own back on Galloping Foxley. Would you have done the same in his situation?

Further activity

Write your own story about a school pupil who is the victim of bullying. The details of your story may include both real and imagined experiences.

Galloping Foxley

Five days a week, for thirty-six years, I have travelled the eight-twelve train to the City. It is never unduly crowded, and it takes me right in to Cannon Street Station, only an eleven and a half minute walk from the door of my office in Austin Friars.

I have always liked the process of commuting; every phase of the little journey is a pleasure to me. There is a regularity about it that is agreeable and comforting to a person of habit, and in addition, it serves as a sort of slipway along which I am gently but firmly launched into the waters of daily business routine.

Ours is a smallish country station and only nineteen or twenty people gather there to catch the eight-twelve. We are a group that rarely changes, and when occasionally a new face appears on the platform it causes a certain disclamatory, protestant ripple, like a new bird in a cage of canaries.

But normally, when I arrive in the morning with my usual four minutes to spare, there they all are, these good, solid, steadfast people, standing in their right places with their right umbrellas and hats and ties and faces and their newspapers under their arms, as unchanged and unchangeable through the years as the furniture in my own living-room. I like that.

I like also my corner seat by the window and reading *The Times* to the noise and motion of the train. This part of it lasts thirty-two minutes and it seems to soothe both my brain and my fretful old body like a good long massage. Believe me, there's nothing like routine and regularity for preserving one's peace of mind. I have now made this morning journey nearly ten thousand times in all, and I enjoy it more and more every day. Also (irrelevant, but interesting), I have become a sort of clock. I can tell at once if we are running two, three, or four minutes late, and I never have to look up to know which station we are stopped at.

The walk at the other end from Cannon Street to my office is neither too long nor too short – a healthy little perambulation along streets crowded with fellow commuters all proceeding to their places of work on the same orderly schedule as myself. It gives me a sense of assurance to be moving among these dependable, dignified people who stick to their jobs and don't go gadding about all over the world. Their lives, like my own, are regulated nicely by the minute hand of an accurate watch, and very often our paths cross at the same times and places on the street each day.

For example, as I turn the corner into St Swithin's Lane, I invariably come head on with a genteel middle-aged lady who wears silver pince-nez and carries a black brief-case in her hand – a first-rate accountant, I should say, or possibly an executive in the textile industry. When I cross over Threadneedle Street by the traffic lights, nine times out of ten I pass a gentleman who wears a different garden flower in his buttonhole each day. He dresses in black trousers and grey spats and is clearly a punctual and meticulous person, probably a banker, or perhaps a solicitor like myself; and several times in the last twenty-five years, as we have hurried past one another across the street, our eyes have met in a fleeting glance of mutual approval and respect.

At least half the faces I pass on this little walk are now familiar to me. And good faces they are too, my kind of faces, my kind of people – sound, sedulous, businesslike folk with none of that restlessness and glittering eye about them that you see in all these so-called clever types who want to tip the world upside-down with their Labour Governments and socialised medicines and all the rest of it.

So you can see that I am, in every sense of the word, a contented commuter. Or would it be more accurate to say that I *was* a contented commuter? At the time when I wrote the little autobiographical sketch you have just read – intending to circulate it among the staff of my office as an exhortation and an example – I was giving a perfectly true account of my feelings.

But that was a whole week ago, and since then something rather peculiar has happened. As a matter of fact, it started to happen last Tuesday, the very morning that I was carrying the rough draft up to town in my pocket; and this, to me, was so timely and coincidental that I can only believe it to have been the work of God. God had read my little essay and he had said to himself, 'This man Perkins is becoming over-complacent. It is high time I taught him a lesson.' I honestly believe that's what happened.

As I say, it was last Tuesday, the Tuesday after Easter, a warm yellow spring morning, and I was striding on to the platform of our small country station with *The Times* tucked under my arm and the draft of 'The Contented Commuter' in my pocket, when I immediately became aware that something was wrong. I could actually *feel* that curious little ripple of protest running along the ranks of my fellow commuters. I stopped and glanced around.

The stranger was standing plumb in the middle of the platform, feet apart and arms folded, looking for all the world as though he owned the whole place. He was a biggish, thickset man, and even from behind he somehow managed to convey a powerful impression of arrogance and oil. Very definitely, he was not one of us. He carried a cane instead of an umbrella, his shoes were brown instead of black, the grey hat was cocked at a ridiculous angle, and in one way and another there seemed to be an excess of silk and polish about his person. More than this I did not care to observe. I walked straight past him with my face to the sky, adding, I sincerely hope, a touch of real frost to an atmosphere that was already cool.

The train came in. And now, try if you can to imagine my horror when the new man actually followed me into *my own* compartment! Nobody had done this to me for fifteen years. My colleagues always respect my seniority. One of my special little pleasures is to have the place to myself for at least one, sometimes two or even three stations. But here, if you please, was this fellow, this stranger, straddling the seat opposite and blowing his nose and rustling the *Daily Mail* and lighting a disgusting pipe.

I lowered my *Times* and stole a glance at his knee. I suppose he was about the same age as me – sixty-two or three – but he had one of those unpleasantly handsome, brown, leathery countenances that you see nowadays in advertisements for men's shirts – the lion shooter and the polo player and the Everest climber and the tropical explorer and the racing yachtsman all rolled into one; dark eyebrows, steely eyes, strong white teeth clamping the stem of a pipe. Personally, I mistrust all handsome men. The superficial pleasures of this life come too easily to them, and they seem to walk the world as though they themselves were personally responsible for their own good looks. I don't mind a *woman* being pretty. That's different. But in a man, I'm sorry, but somehow or other I find it downright offensive. Anyway, here was this one sitting right opposite me in the carriage, and I was looking at him over the top of my *Times* when suddenly he glanced up and our eyes met.

'D'you mind the pipe?' he asked, holding it up in his fingers. That was all he said. But the sound of his voice had a sudden and extraordinary effect upon me. In fact, I think I jumped. Then I sort of froze up and sat staring at him for at least a minute before I got a hold of myself and made an answer.

'This is a smoker,' I said, 'so you may do as you please.'

'I just thought I'd ask.'

There it was again, that curiously crisp, familiar voice, clipping its words and spitting them out very hard and small like a little quick-firing gun shooting out raspberry seeds. Where had I heard it before? And why did every word seem to strike upon some tiny tender spot far back in my memory?

Good heavens, I thought. Pull yourself together. What sort of nonsense is this?

The stranger returned to his paper. I pretended to do the same. But by this time I was properly put out and I couldn't concentrate at all. Instead, I kept stealing glances at him over the top of the editorial page. It was really an intolerable face, vulgarly, almost lasciviously handsome, with an oily salacious sheen all over the skin. But had I or had I not seen it before some time in my life? I began to think I had, because now, even when I looked at it I felt a peculiar kind of discomfort that I cannot quite describe – something to do with pain and with violence, perhaps even with fear.

We spoke no more during the journey, but you can well imagine that by then my whole routine had been thoroughly upset. My day was ruined; and more than one of my clerks at the office felt the sharper edge of my tongue, particularly after luncheon when my digestion started acting up on me as well.

The next morning, there he was again standing in the middle of the platform with his cane and his pipe and his silk scarf and his nauseatingly handsome face. I walked past him and approached a certain Mr Grummitt, a stockbroker who has been commuting with me for over twenty-eight years. I can't say I've ever had an actual conversation with him before – we are rather a reserved lot on our station – but a crisis like this will usually break the ice.

'Grummitt,' I whispered. 'Who's this bounder?'

'Search me,' Grummitt said.

'Pretty unpleasant.'

'Very.'

'Not going to be a regular, I trust.'

'Oh God,' Grummitt said.

Then the train came in.

This time, to my great relief, the man got into another compartment.

But the following morning I had him with me again.

'Well,' he said, settling back in the seat directly opposite. 'It's a *topping* day.' And once again I felt that slow uneasy stirring of the memory, stronger than ever this time, closer to the surface but not yet quite within my reach.

Then came Friday, the last day of the week. I remember it had rained as I drove to the station, but it was one of those warm sparkling April showers that last only five or six minutes, and when I walked on to the platform, all the umbrellas were rolled up and the sun was shining and there were big white clouds floating in the sky. In spite of this, I felt depressed. There was no pleasure in this journey for me any longer. I knew the stranger would be there. And sure enough, he was, standing with his legs apart just as though he owned the place, and this time swinging his cane casually back and forth through the air.

The cane! That did it! I stopped like I'd been shot.

'It's Foxley!' I cried under my breath. 'Galloping Foxley! And still swinging his cane!'

I stepped closer to get a better look. I tell you I've never had such a shock in all my life. It was Foxley all right. Bruce Foxley or Galloping Foxley as we used to call him. And the last time I'd seen him, let me see – it was at school and I was no more than twelve or thirteen years old.

At that point the train came in, and heaven help me if he didn't get into my compartment once again. He put his hat and cane up on the rack, then turned and sat down and began lighting his pipe. He glanced up at me through the smoke with those rather small cold eyes and he said, '*Ripping* day, isn't it. Just like summer.'

There was no mistaking the voice now. It hadn't changed at all. Except that the things I had been used to hearing it say were different.

'All right, Perkins,' it used to say. 'All right, you nasty little boy. I am about to beat you again.'

How long ago was that? It must be nearly fifty years. Extraordinary, though, how little the features had altered. Still the same arrogant tilt of the chin, the flaring nostrils, the contemptuous staring eyes that were too small and a shade too close together for comfort; still the same habit of thrusting his face forward at you, impinging on you, pushing you into a corner; and even the hair I could remember – coarse and slightly wavy, with just a trace of oil all over it, like a well-tossed salad. He used to keep a bottle of green hair mixture on the side table in his study – when you have to dust a room you get to know and to hate all the objects in it and this bottle had the royal coat of arms on the label and the name of a shop in Bond Street, and under that, in small print, it said 'By Appointment – Hairdressers To His Majesty King Edward VII.' I can remember that particularly because it seemed so funny that a shop should want to boast about being hairdresser to someone who was practically bald – even a monarch.

And now I watched Foxley settle back in his seat and begin reading the paper. It was a curious sensation, sitting only a yard away from this man who fifty years before had made me so miserable that I had once contemplated suicide. He hadn't recognised *me;* there wasn't much danger of that because of my moustache. I felt fairly sure I was safe and could sit there and watch him all I wanted.

Looking back on it, there seems little doubt that I suffered very badly at the hands of Bruce Foxley my first year in school, and strangely enough, the unwitting cause of it all was my father. I was twelve and a half when I first went off to this fine old public school. That was, let me see, in 1907. My father, who wore a silk topper and morning coat, escorted me to the station, and I can remember how we were standing on the platform among piles of wooden tuck-boxes and trunks and what seemed like thousands of very large boys milling about and talking and shouting at one another, when suddenly somebody who was wanting to get by us gave my father a great push from behind and nearly knocked him off his feet.

My father, who was a small, courteous, dignified person, turned around with surprising speed and seized the culprit by the wrist.

'Don't they teach you better manners than that at this school, young man?' he said.

The boy, at least a head taller than my father, looked down at him with a cold, arrogant-laughing glare, and said nothing.

'It seems to me,' my father said, staring back at him, 'that an apology would be in order.'

But the boy just kept on looking down his nose at my father with this funny little arrogant smile at the corners of his mouth, and his chin kept coming further and further out.

'You strike me as being an impudent and ill-mannered boy,' my father went on. 'And I can only pray that you are an exception in your school. I would not wish for any son of mine to pick up such habits.'

At this point, the big boy inclined his head slightly in my direction, and a pair of small, cold, rather close together eyes looked down into mine. I was not particularly frightened at the time; I knew nothing about the power of senior boys over junior boys at public schools; and I can remember that I looked straight back at him in support of my father, whom I adored and respected.

When my father started to say something more, the boy simply turned away and sauntered slowly down the platform into the crowd.

Bruce Foxley never forgot this episode; and of course the really unlucky thing about it for me was that when I arrived at school I found myself in the same 'house' as him. Even worse than that – I was in his study. He was doing his last year, and he was a prefect – 'a boazer' we called it – and as such he was officially permitted to beat any of the fags in the house. But being in his study, I automatically became his own particular, personal slave. I was his valet and cook and maid and errand-boy, and it was my duty to see that he never lifted a finger for himself unless absolutely necessary. In no society that I know of in the world is a servant imposed upon to the extent that we wretched little fags were imposed upon by the boazers at school. In frosty or snowy weather I even had to sit on the seat of the lavatory (which was in an unheated outhouse) every morning after breakfast to warm it before Foxley came along.

I could remember how he used to saunter across the room in his loose-jointed, elegant way, and if a chair were in his path he would knock it aside and I would have to run over and pick it up. He wore silk shirts and always had a silk handkerchief tucked up his sleeve, and his shoes were made by someone called Lobb (who also had a royal crest). They were pointed shoes, and it was my duty to rub the leather with a bone for fifteen minutes each day to make it shine.

But the worst memories of all had to do with the changing-room.

I could see myself now, a small pale shrimp of a boy standing just inside the door of this huge room in my pyjamas and bedroom slippers and brown camel-hair dressing-gown. A single bright electric bulb was hanging on a flex from the ceiling, and all around the walls the black and yellow football shirts with their sweaty smell filling the room, and the voice, the clipped, pip-spitting voice was saying, 'So which is it to be this time? Six with the dressing gown on – or four with it off?'

I never could bring myself to answer this question. I would simply stand there staring down at the dirty floor-planks, dizzy with fear and unable to think of anything except that this other larger boy would soon start smashing away at me with his long, thin, white stick, slowly, scientifically, skilfully, legally, and with apparent relish, and I would bleed. Five hours earlier, I had failed to get the fire to light in his study. I had spent my pocket money on a box of special firelighters and I had held a newspaper across the chimney opening to make a draught and I had knelt down in front of it and blown my guts out into the bottom of the grate; but the coals would not burn.

'If you're too obstinate to answer,' the voice was saying, 'then I'll have to decide for you.'

I wanted desperately to answer because I knew which one I had to choose. It's the first thing you learn when you arrive. Always keep the dressing-gown *on* and take the extra strokes.

Otherwise you're almost certain to get cut. Even three with it on is better than one with it off.

'Take it off then and get into the far corner and touch your toes. I'm going to give you four.'

Slowly I would take it off and lay it on the ledge above the boot-lockers. And slowly I would walk over to the far corner, cold and naked now in my cotton pyjamas, treading softly and seeing everything around me suddenly very bright and flat and far away, like a magic lantern picture, and very big, and very unreal, and sort of swimming through the water in my eyes.

'Go on and touch your toes. Tighter – much tighter than that.'

Then he would walk down to the far end of the changing-room and I would be watching him upside down between my legs, and he would disappear through a doorway that led down two steps into what we called 'the basin-passage'. This was a stone-floored corridor with wash basins along one wall, and beyond it was the bathroom. When Foxley disappeared I knew he was walking down to the far end of the basin-passage. Foxley always did that. Then, in the distance, but echoing loud among the basins and the tiles, I would hear the noise of his shoes on the stone floor as he started galloping forward, and through my legs I would see him leaping up the two steps into the changing-room and come bounding towards me with his face thrust forward and the cane held high in the air. This was the moment when I shut my eyes and waited for the crack and told myself that whatever happened I must not straighten up.

Anyone who has been properly beaten will tell you that the real pain does not come until about eight or ten seconds after the stroke. The stroke itself is merely a loud crack and a sort of blunt thud against your backside, numbing you completely (I'm told a bullet wound does the same). But later on, oh my heavens, if feels as if someone is laying a red hot poker right across your naked buttocks and it is absolutely impossible to prevent yourself from reaching back and clutching it with your fingers.

Foxley knew all about this time lag, and the slow walk back over a distance that must altogether have been fifteen yards gave each stroke plenty of time to reach the peak of its pain before the next one was delivered.

On the fourth stroke I would invariably straighten up. I couldn't help it. It was an automatic defence reaction from a body that had had as much as it could stand.

'You flinched,' Foxley would say. 'That one doesn't count. Go on – down you get.'

The next time I would remember to grip my ankles.

Afterwards he would watch me as I walked over – very stiff now and holding my backside – to put on my dressing-gown, but I would always try to keep turned away from him so he couldn't see my face. And when I went out, it would be, 'Hey, you! Come back!'

I was in the passage then, and I would stop and turn and stand in the doorway, waiting.

'Come here. Come on, come back here. Now – haven't you forgotten something?'

All I could think of at that moment was the excruciating burning pain in my behind.

'You strike me as being an impudent and ill-mannered boy,' he would say, imitating my father's voice. 'Don't they teach you better manners than that at this school?'

'Thank … you,' I would stammer. 'Thank … you … for the beating.'

And then back up the dark stairs to the dormitory and it became much better then because it was all over and the pain was going and the others were clustering round and treating me with a certain rough sympathy born of having gone through the same thing themselves, many times.

'Hey, Perkins, let's have a look.'

'How many d'you get?'

'Five, wasn't it? We heard them easily from here.'

'Come on, man. Let's see the marks.'

I would take down my pyjamas and stand there while this group of experts solemnly examined the damage.

'Rather far apart, aren't they? Not quite up to Foxley's usual standard.'

'Two of them are close. Actually touching. Look – these two are beauties!'

'That low one was a rotten shot.'

'Did he go right down the basin-passage to start his run?'

'You got an extra one for flinching, didn't you?'

'By golly, old Foxley's really got it in for *you*, Perkins.'

'Bleeding a bit too. Better wash it, you know.'

Then the door would open and Foxley would be there, and everyone would scatter and pretend to be doing his teeth or saying his prayers while I was left standing in the centre of the room with my pants down.

'What's going on here?' Foxley would say, taking a quick look at his own handiwork. 'You Perkins! Put your pyjamas on properly and get into bed.'

And that was the end of a day.

Through the week, I never had a moment of time to myself. If

Foxley saw me in the study taking up a novel or perhaps opening my stamp album, he would immediately find something for me to do. One of his favourites, especially when it was raining outside, was 'Oh, Perkins, I think a bunch of wild irises would look rather nice on my desk, don't you?'

Wild irises grew only around Orange Ponds. Orange Ponds was two miles down the road and half a mile across the fields. I would get up from my chair, put on my raincoat and my straw hat, take my umbrella – my brolly – and set off on this long and lonely trek. The straw hat had to be worn at all times outdoors, but it was easily destroyed by rain; therefore the brolly was necessary to protect the hat. On the other hand, you can't keep a brolly over your head while scrambling about on a woody bank looking for irises, so to save my hat from ruin I would put it on the ground under my brolly while I searched for flowers. In this way, I caught many colds.

But the most dreaded day was Sunday, Sunday was for cleaning the study, and how well I can remember the terror of those mornings, the frantic dusting and scrubbing, and then the waiting for Foxley to come in to inspect.

'Finished?' he would ask.

'I … think so.'

Then he would stroll over to the drawer of his desk and take out a single white glove, fitting it slowly on to his right hand, pushing each finger well home, and I would stand there watching and trembling as he moved around the room running his white gloved forefinger along the picture tops, the skirting, the shelves, the window sills, the lamp shades. I never took my eyes off that finger. For me it was an instrument of doom. Nearly always, it managed to discover some tiny crack that I had overlooked or perhaps hadn't even thought about; and when this happened Foxley would turn slowly around, smiling that dangerous little smile that wasn't a smile, holding up the white finger so that I should see for myself the thin smudge of dust that lay along the side of it.

'Well,' he would say. 'So you're a lazy little boy. Aren't you?'

No answer.

'Aren't you?'

'I thought I dusted it all.'

'Are you or are you not a nasty, lazy little boy?'

'Y-yes.'

'But your father wouldn't want you to grow up like that, would he? Your father is very particular about manners, is he not?'

No answer.

'I asked you, is your father particular about manners?'

'Perhaps – yes.'

'Therefore I will be doing him a favour if I punish you, won't I?'

'I don't know.'

'Won't I?'

'Y-yes?'

'We will meet later then, after prayers, in the changing-room.'

The rest of the day would be spent in an agony of waiting for the evening to come.

Oh my goodness, how it was all coming back to me now. Sunday was also letter-writing time. 'Dear Mummy and Daddy – thank you very much for your letter. I hope you are both well. I am, except I have got a cold because I got caught in the rain but it will soon be over. Yesterday we played Shrewsbury and beat them 4-2. I watched and Foxley who you know is the head of our house scored one of our goals. Thank you very much for the cake. With love from William.'

I usually went to the lavatory to write my letter, or to the boot-hole, or the bathroom – any place out of Foxley's way. But I had to watch the time. Tea was at four-thirty and Foxley's toast had to be ready. Every day I had to make toast for Foxley, and on weekdays there were no fires allowed in the studies, so all the fags, each making toast for his own studyholder, would have to crowd around the one small fire in the library, jockeying for position with his toasting-fork. Under these conditions, I still had to see that Foxley's toast was (1) very crisp, (2) not burned at all, (3) hot and ready exactly on time. To fail in any one of these requirements was a 'beatable offence'.

'Hey, you! What's this?'

'It's toast.'

'Is this really your idea of toast?'

'Well … '

'You're too idle to make it right, aren't you?'

'I try to make it.'

'You know what they do to an idle horse, Perkins?'

'No,'

'Are you a horse?'

'No.'

'Well – anyway, you're an ass – ha, ha – so I think you qualify. I'll be seeing you later.'

Oh, the agony of those days. To burn Foxley's toast was a 'beatable offence'. So was forgetting to take the mud off Foxley's football boots. So was failing to hang up Foxley's football clothes. So was rolling up Foxley's brolly the wrong way round. So was banging the study door when Foxley was working. So was filling Foxley's bath too hot for him. So was not cleaning the buttons properly on Foxley's OTC uniform. So was making those blue metal-polish smudges on the uniform itself. So was failing to shine the *soles* of Foxley's shoes. So was leaving Foxley's study untidy at any time. In fact, so far as Foxley was concerned, I was practically a beatable offence myself.

I glanced out of the window. My goodness, we were nearly there. I must have been dreaming away like this for quite a while, and I hadn't even opened my *Times*. Foxley was still leaning back in the corner seat opposite me reading his *Daily*

Mail, and through a cloud of blue smoke from his pipe I could see the top half of his face over the newspaper, the small bright eyes, the corrugated forehead, the wavy, slightly oily hair.

Looking at him now, after all that time, was a peculiar and rather exciting experience. I knew he was no longer dangerous, but the old memories were still there and I didn't feel altogether comfortable in his presence. It was something like being inside the cage with a tame tiger.

What nonsense is this? I asked myself. Don't be so stupid. My heavens, if you wanted to you could go ahead and tell him exactly what you thought of him and he couldn't touch you. Hey that was an idea!

Except that – well – after all, was it worth it? I was too old for that sort of thing now, and I wasn't sure that I really felt much anger towards him anyway.

So what should I do? I couldn't sit there staring at him like an idiot.

At that point, a little impish fancy began to take a hold of me. What I would like to do, I told myself, would be to lean across and tap him lightly on the knee and tell him who I was. Then I would watch his face. After that, I would begin talking about our schooldays together, making it just loud enough for the other people in the carriage to hear. I would remind him playfully of some of the things he used to do to me, and perhaps even describe the changing-room beatings so as to embarrass him a trifle. A bit of teasing and discomfort wouldn't do him any harm. And it would do *me* an awful lot of good.

Suddenly he glanced up and caught me staring at him. It was the second time this had happened, and I noticed a flicker of irritation in his eyes.

All right, I told myself. Here we go. But keep it pleasant and sociable and polite. It'll be much more effective that way, more embarrassing for him.

So I smiled at him and gave him a courteous little nod. Then, raising my voice, I said, 'I do hope you'll excuse me. I'd like to introduce myself.' I was leaning forward watching him closely so as not to miss the reaction. 'My name is Perkins – William Perkins – and I was at Repton in 1907.'

The others in the carriage were sitting very still, and I could sense that they were all listening and waiting to see what would happen next.

'I'm glad to meet you,' he said, lowering the paper to his lap. 'Mine's Fortescue – Jocelyn Fortescue. Eton, 1916.'

Notes on Mrs Bixby and the Colonel's Coat

This story covers a variety of themes that the writer considers are relevant to modern life. It is about greed, deceit and vanity. Roald Dahl adds the further dimension of justice, as he is keen to point out that whatever wrongs we commit in this life will eventually catch up with us.

What do you think?

We know throughout this story that the wronged husband will turn the tables on his unfaithful wife. There are certain aspects to the story which contribute to the sense of satisfaction we feel that Mrs Bixby has received her just desserts. As you read, consider:

- Mrs Bixby's real reasons for going to visit her aunt
- her reaction to the colonel's letter and his present of the coat
- her attitude towards her husband and her marriage
- whether your sympathies towards Mr Bixby have changed.

Questions

Look for key passages in the text that provide evidence to support your answers to these questions:

1. Describe and explain the writer's attitude towards American women.

2. Pick out words and phrases that show that Mrs Bixby likes her fur coat.

3. Why does Mrs Bixby take her fur coat to the pawnbrokers? What does Mrs Bixby's plan suggest about her?

4. How does Roald Dahl develop suspense and the reader's expectations within the story?

5. Who do we feel the most sympathy towards at the end of the story, Mr or Mrs Bixby? Explain the reasons for your answer.

Further activity

Write a script in which Mr Bixby describes his version of the events surrounding the fur coat to one of his close friends. In your script explain:

- Mr Bixby's attitude towards his wife
- his relationship with his secretary Miss Pulteney
- how and why Miss Pulteney ended up with the fur coat.

Mrs Bixby and the Colonel's Coat

America is the land of opportunities for women. Already they own about eighty-five per cent of the wealth of the nation. Soon they will have it all. Divorce has become a lucrative process, simple to arrange and easy to forget; and ambitious females can repeat it as often as they please and parlay their winnings to astronomical figures. The husband's death also brings satisfactory rewards and some ladies prefer to rely upon this method. They know that the waiting period will not be unduly protracted, for overwork and hypertension are bound to get the poor devil before long, and he will die at his desk with a bottle of benzedrines in one hand and a packet of tranquillisers in the other.

Succeeding generations of youthful American males are not deterred in the slightest by this terrifying pattern of divorce and death. The higher the divorce rate climbs, the more eager they become. Young men marry like mice, almost before they have reached the age of puberty, and a large proportion of them have at least two ex-wives on the payroll by the time they are thirty-six years old. To support these ladies in the manner to which they are accustomed, the men must work like slaves, which is of course precisely what they are. But now at last, as they approach their premature middle age, a sense of disillusionment and fear begins to creep slowly into their hearts, and in the evenings they take to huddling together in little groups, in clubs and bars, drinking their whiskies and swallowing their pills, and trying to comfort one another with stories.

The basic theme of these stories never varies. There are always three main characters – the husband, the wife, and the dirty dog. The husband is a decent clean-living man, working hard at his job. The wife is cunning, deceitful, and lecherous, and she is invariably up to some sort of jiggery-pokery with the dirty dog. The husband is too good a man even to suspect her. Things look black for the husband. Will the poor man ever find out? Must he be a cuckold for the rest of his life? Yes, he must. But wait! Suddenly, by a brilliant manoeuvre, the husband completely turns the tables on his monstrous spouse. The woman is flabbergasted, stupefied, humiliated, defeated. The audience of men around the bar smiles quietly to itself and takes a little comfort from the fantasy.

There are many of these stories going around,. these wonderful wishful-thinking dreamworld inventions of the unhappy male, but most of them are too fatuous to be worth repeating, and far too fruity to be put down on paper. There is one, however, that seems to be superior to the rest, particularly as it has the merit of being true. It is extremely popular with twice- or thrice-bitten males in search of solace, and if you are one of them, and if you haven't heard it before, you may enjoy the way it comes out. The story is called 'Mrs Bixby and the Colonel's Coat', and it goes something like this:

Mr and Mrs Bixby lived in a smallish apartment somewhere in New York City. Mr Bixby was a dentist who made an average income. Mrs Bixby was a big vigorous woman with a wet mouth. Once a month, always on Friday afternoons, Mrs Bixby would board the train at Pennsylvania Station and travel to Baltimore to visit her old aunt. She would spend the night with the aunt and return to New York on the following day in time to cook supper for her husband. Mr Bixby accepted this arrangement goodnaturedly. He knew that Aunt Maude lived in Baltimore, and that his wife was very fond of the old lady, and certainly it would be unreasonable to deny either of them the pleasure of a monthly meeting.

'Just so long as you don't ever expect me to accompany you,' Mr Bixby had said in the beginning.

'Of course not, darling,' Mrs Bixby had answered. 'After all, she is not your aunt. She's mine.'

104

So far so good.

As it turned out, however, the aunt was little more than a convenient alibi for Mrs Bixby. The dirty dog, in the shape of a gentleman known as the Colonel, was lurking slyly in the background, and our heroine spent the greater part of her Baltimore time in this scoundrel's company. The Colonel was exceedingly wealthy. He lived in a charming house on the outskirts of the town. No wife or family encumbered him, only a few discreet and loyal servants, and in Mrs Bixby's absence he consoled himself by riding his horses and hunting the fox.

Year after year, this pleasant alliance between Mrs Bixby and the Colonel continued without a hitch. They met so seldom – twelve times a year is not much when you come to think of it – that there was little or no chance of their growing bored with one another. On the contrary, the long wait between meetings only made the heart grow fonder, and each separate occasion became an exciting reunion.

'Tally-ho!' the Colonel would cry each time he met her at the station in the big car. 'My dear, I'd almost forgotten how ravishing you looked. Let's go to earth.'

Eight years went by.

It was just before Christmas, and Mrs Bixby was standing on the station in Baltimore waiting for the train to take her back to New York. This particular visit which had just ended had been more than usually agreeable, and she was in a cheerful mood. But then the Colonel's company always did that to her these days. The man had a way of making her feel that she was altogether a rather remarkable woman, a person of subtle and exotic talents, fascinating beyond measure; and what a very different thing that was from the dentist husband at home who never succeeded in making her feel that she was anything but a sort of eternal patient, someone who dwelt in the waiting-room, silent among the magazines, seldom if ever nowadays to be called in to suffer the finicky precise ministrations of those clean pink hands.

'The Colonel asked me to give you this,' a voice beside her said. She turned and saw Wilkins, the Colonel's groom, a small wizened dwarf with grey skin, and he was pushing a large flattish cardboard box into her arms.

'Good gracious me!' she cried, all of a flutter. 'My heavens, what an enormous box! What is it, Wilkins? Was there a message? Did he send me a message?'

'No message,' the groom said, and he walked away.

As soon as she was on the train, Mrs Bixby carried the box into the privacy of the Ladies' Room and locked the door. How exciting this was! A Christmas present from the Colonel. She started to undo the string. 'I'll bet it's a dress,' she said aloud. 'It might even be two dresses. Or it might be a whole lot of beautiful underclothes. I won't look. I'll just feel around and try to guess what it is. I'll try to guess the colour as well, and exactly what it looks like. Also how much it cost.'

She shut her eyes tight and slowly lifted off the lid. Then she put one hand down into the box. There was some tissue paper on top; she could feel it and hear it rustling. There was also an envelope or a card of some sort. She ignored this and began burrowing underneath the tissue paper, the fingers reaching out delicately, like tendrils.

'My God,' she cried suddenly. 'It can't be true!'

She opened her eyes wide and stared at the coat. Then she pounced on it and lifted it out of the box. Thick layers of fur made a lovely noise against the tissue paper as they unfolded, and when she held it up and saw it hanging to its full length, it was so beautiful it took her breath away.

Never had she seen mink like this before. It *was* mink, wasn't it? Yes, of course it was. But what a glorious colour! The fur was almost pure black. At first she thought it *was* black; but when she held it closer to the window she saw that there was a touch of blue in it as well, a deep rich blue, like cobalt. Quickly she looked at the label. It said simply, WILD LABRADOR MINK. There was nothing else, no sign of where it had been bought or anything. But that, she told herself, was probably the Colonel's doing. The wily old fox was making darn sure he didn't leave any tracks. Good for him. But what in the world could it have cost? She hardly dared to think. Four, five, six thousand dollars? Possibly more.

She just couldn't take her eyes off it. Nor, for that matter, could she wait to try it on. Quickly she slipped off her own plain red coat. She was panting a little now, she couldn't help it, and her eyes were stretched very wide. But oh God, the feel of that fur! And those huge wide sleeves with their thick turned-up cuffs! Who was it had once told her that they always used female skins for the arms and male skins for the rest of the coat? Someone had told her that. Joan Rutfield, probably; though how *Joan* would know anything about *mink* she couldn't imagine.

The great black coat seemed to slide on to her almost of its own accord, like a second skin. Oh boy! It was the queerest feeling! She glanced into the mirror. It was fantastic. Her whole personality had suddenly changed completely. She looked dazzling, radiant, rich, brilliant, voluptuous, all at the same time.

And the sense of power that it gave her! In this coat she could walk into any place she wanted and people would come scurrying around her like rabbits. The whole thing was just too wonderful for words!

Mrs Bixby picked up the envelope that was still lying in the box. She opened it and pulled out the Colonel's letter:

I once heard you saying you were fond of mink so I got you this. I'm told it's a good one. Please accept it with my sincere good wishes as a parting gift. For my own personal reasons I shall not be able to see you any more. Good-bye and good luck.

Well!

Imagine that!

Right out of the blue, just when she was feeling so happy.

No more Colonel.

What a dreadful shock.

She would miss him enormously.

Slowly, Mrs Bixby began stroking the lovely soft black fur of the coat.

What you lose on the swings you get back on the roundabouts.

She smiled and folded the letter, meaning to tear it up and throw it out of the window, but in folding it she noticed that there was something written on the other side:

P.S. just tell them that nice generous aunt of yours gave it to you for Christmas.

Mrs Bixby's mouth, at that moment stretched wide in a silky smile, snapped back like a piece of elastic.

'The man must be mad!' she cried. 'Aunt Maude doesn't have that sort of money. She couldn't possibly give me this.'

But if Aunt Maude didn't give it to her, then who did?

Oh God! In the excitement of finding the coat and trying it on, she had completely overlooked this vital aspect.

In a couple of hours she would be in New York. Ten minutes after that she would be home, and the husband would be there to greet her; and even a man like Cyril, dwelling as he did in a dark phlegmy world of root canals, bicuspids, and caries, would start asking a few questions if his wife suddenly waltzed in from a week-end wearing a six-thousand-dollar mink coat.

You know what I think, she told herself. I think that goddamn Colonel has done this on purpose just to torture me. He knew perfectly well Aunt Maude didn't have enough money to buy this. He knew I wouldn't be able to keep it.

But the thought of parting with it now was more than Mrs Bixby could bear.

'I've *got* to have this coat!' she said aloud. 'I've got to have this coat! I've got to have this coat!'

Very well, my dear. You shall have the coat. But don't panic. Sit still and keep calm and start thinking. You're a clever girl, aren't you? You've fooled him before. The man never has been able to see much further than the end of his own probe, you know that. So just sit absolutely still and *think*. There's lots of time.

Two and a half hours later, Mrs Bixby stepped off the train at Pennsylvania Station and walked quickly to the exit. She was wearing her old red coat again now and carrying the cardboard box in her arms. She signalled for a taxi.

'Driver,' she said, 'would you know of a pawnbroker that's still open around here?'

The man behind the wheel raised his brows and looked back at her, amused.

'Plenty along Sixth Avenue,' he answered.

'Stop at the first one you see, then, will you please?' She got in and was driven away.

Soon the taxi pulled up outside a shop that had three brass balls hanging over the entrance.

'Wait for me, please,' Mrs Bixby, said to the driver, and she got out of the taxi and entered the shop.

There was an enormous cat crouching on the counter eating fishheads out of a white saucer. The animal looked up at Mrs Bixby with bright yellow eyes, then looked away again and went on eating. Mrs Bixby stood by the counter, as far away from the cat as possible, waiting for someone to come, staring at the watches, the shoe buckles, the enamel brooches, the old binoculars, the broken spectacles, the false teeth. Why did they always pawn their teeth, she wondered.

'Yes?' the proprietor said, emerging from a dark place in the back of the shop.

'Oh, good evening,' Mrs Bixby said. She began to untie the string around the box. The man went up to the cat and started stroking it along the top of its back, and the cat went on eating the fishheads.

'Isn't it silly of me?' Mrs Bixby said. 'I've gone and lost my pocketbook, and this being Saturday, the banks are all closed until Monday and I've simply got to have some money for the week-end. This is quite a valuable coat, but I'm not asking much. I only want to borrow enough on it to tide me over till Monday. Then I'll come back and redeem it.'

The man waited, and said nothing. But when she pulled out the mink and allowed the beautiful thick fur to fall over the counter, his eyebrows went up and he drew his hand away from the cat and came over to look at it. He picked it up and held it out in front of him.

'If only I had a watch on me or a ring,' Mrs Bixby said, 'I'd give you that instead. But the fact is I don't have a thing with me other than this coat.' She spread out her fingers for him to see.

'It looks new,' the man said, fondling the soft fur.

'Oh yes, it is. But, as I said, I only want to borrow enough to tide me over till Monday. How about fifty dollars?'

'I'll loan you fifty dollars.'

'It's worth a hundred times more than that, but I know you'll take good care of it until I return.'

The man went over to a drawer and fetched a ticket and placed it on the counter. The ticket looked like one of those labels you tie on to the handle of your suitcase, the same shape and size exactly, and the same stiff brownish paper. But it was perforated across the middle so that you could tear it in two, and both halves were identical.

'Name?' he asked.

'Leave that out. And the address.'

She saw the man pause, and she saw the nib of the pen hovering over the dotted line, waiting.

'You don't *have* to put the name and address, do you?'

The man shrugged and shook his head and the pen-nib moved on down to the next line.

'It's just that I'd rather not,' Mrs Bixby said. 'It's purely personal.'

'You'd better not lose this ticket, then.'

'I won't lose it.'

'You realise that anyone who gets hold of it can come in and claim the article?'

'Yes, I know that.'

'Simply on the number.'

'Yes, I know.'

'What do you want me to put for a description.'

'No description either, thank you. It's not necessary. Just put the amount I'm borrowing.'

The pen-nib hesitated again, hovering over the dotted line beside the word ARTICLE.

'I think you ought to put a description. A description is always a help if you want to sell the ticket. You never know, you might want to sell it sometime.'

'I don't want to sell it.'

'You might have to. Lots of people do.'

'Look,' Mrs Bixby said. 'I'm not broke, if that's what you mean. I simply lost my purse. Don't you understand?'

'You have it your own way then,' the man said. 'It's your coat.'

At this point an unpleasant thought struck Mrs Bixby. 'Tell me something,' she said. 'If I don't have a description on my ticket, how can I be sure you'll give me back the coat and not something else when I return?'

'It goes in the books.'

'But all I've got is a number. So actually you could hand me any old thing you wanted, isn't that so?'

'Do you want a description or don't you?' the man asked.

'No,' she said. 'I trust you.'

The man wrote 'fifty dollars' opposite the word VALUE on both sections of the ticket, then he tore it in half along the perforations and slid the lower portion across the counter. He took a wallet from the inside pocket of his jacket and extracted five ten-dollar bills. 'The interest is three per cent a month,' he said.

'Yes, all right. And thank you. You'll take good care of it, won't you?'

The man nodded but said nothing.

'Shall I put it back in the box for you?'

'No,' the man said.

Mrs Bixby turned and went out of the shop on to the street where the taxi was waiting. Ten minutes later, she was home.

'Darling,' she said as she bent over and kissed her husband. 'Did you miss me?'

Cyril Bixby laid down the evening paper and glanced at the watch on his wrist. 'It's twelve and a half minutes past six,' he said. 'You're a bit late, aren't you?'

'I know. It's those dreadful trains. Aunt Maude sent you her love as usual. I'm dying for a drink, aren't you?'

The husband folded his newspaper into a neat rectangle and placed it on the arm of his chair. Then he stood up and crossed over to the sideboard. His wife remained in the centre of the room pulling off her gloves, watching him carefully, wondering how long she ought to wait. He had his back to her now, bending forward to measure the gin, putting his face right up close to the measurer and peering into it as though it were a patient's mouth.

It was funny how small he always looked after the Colonel. The Colonel was huge and bristly, and when you were near to him he smelled faintly of horseradish. This one was small and neat and bony and he didn't really smell of anything at all, except peppermint drops, which he sucked to keep his breath nice for the patients.

'See what I've brought for measuring the vermouth,' he said, holding up a calibrated glass beaker. 'I can get it to the nearest milligram with this.'

'Darling, how clever.'

I really must try to make him change the way he dresses, she told herself. His suits are just too ridiculous for words. There had been a time when she thought they were wonderful, those Edwardian jackets with high lapels and six buttons down the front, but now they merely seemed absurd. So did the narrow stovepipe trousers. You had to have a special sort of face to wear things like that, and Cyril just didn't have it. His was a long bony countenance with a narrow nose and a slightly prognathous jaw, and when you saw it coming up out of the top of one of those tightly fitting old-fashioned suits it looked like a caricature of Sam Weller. He probably thought it looked like Beau Brummel. It was a fact that in the office he invariably greeted female patients with his white coat unbuttoned so that they would catch a glimpse of the trappings underneath; and in some obscure way this was obviously meant to convey the impression that he was a bit of a dog. But Mrs Bixby knew better. The plumage was a bluff. It meant nothing. It reminded her of an ageing peacock strutting on the lawn with only half its feathers left. Or one of those fatuous self-fertilising flowers – like the dandelion.

A dandelion never has to get fertilised for the setting of its seed, and all those brilliant yellow petals are just a waste of time, a boast, a masquerade. What's the word the biologists use? Subsexual. A dandelion is subsexual. So, for that matter, are the summer broods of water fleas. It sounds a bit like Lewis Carroll, she thought – water fleas and dandelions and dentists.

'Thank you, darling,' she said, taking the martini and seating herself on the sofa with her handbag on her lap. 'And what did you do last night?'

113

'I stayed on in the office and cast a few inlays. I also got my accounts up to date.'

'Now really, Cyril, I think it's high time you let other people do your donkey work for you. You're much too important for that sort of thing. Why don't you give the inlays to the mechanic?'

'I prefer to do them myself. I'm extremely proud of my inlays.'

'I know you are, darling, and I think they're absolutely wonderful. They're the best inlays in the whole world. But I don't want you to burn yourself out. And why doesn't that Pulteney woman do the accounts? That's part of her job, isn't it?'

'She does do them. But I have to price everything up first. She doesn't know who's rich and who isn't.'

'This Martini is perfect,' Mrs Bixby said, setting down her glass on the side table. 'Quite perfect.' She opened her bag and took out a handkerchief as if to blow her nose. 'Oh look!' she cried, seeing the ticket. 'I forgot to show you this! I found it just now on the seat of my taxi. It's got a number on it, and I thought it might be a lottery ticket or something, so I kept it.'

She handed the small piece of stiff brown paper to her husband, who took it in his fingers and began examining it minutely from all angles, as though it were a suspect tooth.

'You know what this is?' he said slowly.

'No dear, I don't.'

'It's a pawn ticket.'

'A what?'

'A ticket from a pawnbroker. Here's the name and address of the shop somewhere on Sixth Avenue.'

'Oh dear, I *am* disappointed. I was hoping it might be a ticket for the Irish Sweep.'

'There's no reason to be disappointed,' Cyril Bixby said. 'As a matter of fact this could be rather amusing.'

'Why could it be amusing, darling?'

He began explaining to her exactly how a pawn ticket worked, with particular reference to the fact that anyone possessing the ticket was entitled to claim the article. She listened patiently until he had finished his lecture.

'You think it's worth claiming?' she asked.

'I think it's worth finding out what it is. You see this figure of fifty dollars that's written here? You know what that means?'

'No, dear, what does it mean?'

'It means that the item in question is almost certain to be something quite valuable.'

'You mean it'll be worth fifty dollars?'

'More like five hundred.'

'Five hundred!'

'Don't you understand?' he said. 'A pawnbroker never gives you more than about a tenth of the real value.'

'Good gracious! I never knew that.'

'There's a lot of things you don't know, my dear. Now you listen to me. Seeing that there's no name and address of the owner … '

'But surely there's something to say who it belongs to?'

'Not a thing. People often do that. They don't want anyone to know they've been to a pawnbroker. They're ashamed of it.'

'Then you think we can keep it?'

'Of course we can keep it. This is now *our* ticket.'

'You mean *my* ticket,' Mrs Bixby said firmly. 'I found it.'

'My dear girl, what *does* it matter? The important thing is that we are now in a position to go and redeem it any time we like for only fifty dollars. How about that?'

'Oh, what fun!' she cried. 'I think it's terribly exciting, especially when we don't even know what it is. It could be *anything*, isn't that right, Cyril? Absolutely anything!'

'It could indeed, although it's most likely to be either a ring or a watch.'

'But wouldn't it be marvellous if it was a *real* treasure? I mean something *really* old, like a wonderful old vase or a Roman statue.'

'There's no knowing what it might be, my dear. We shall just have to wait and see.'

'I think it's absolutely fascinating! Give me the ticket and I'll rush over first thing Monday morning and find out!'

'I think I'd better do that.'

'Oh no!' she cried. 'Let *me* do it!'

'I think not. I'll pick it up on my way to work.'

'But it's *my* ticket! *Please* let me do it, Cyril! Why should you have all the fun?'

'You don't know these pawnbrokers, my dear. You're liable to get cheated.'

'I wouldn't get cheated, honestly I wouldn't. Give it to me, please.'

'Also you have to have fifty dollars,' he said, smiling. 'You have to pay out fifty dollars in cash before they'll give it to you.'

'I've got that,' she said. 'I think.'

'I'd rather you didn't handle it, if you don't mind.'

'But Cyril, I *found* it. It's mine. Whatever it is, it's mine isn't that right?'

'Of course it's yours, my dear. There's no need to get so worked up about it.'

'I'm not. I'm just excited, that's all.'

'I suppose it hasn't occurred to you that this might be something entirely masculine – a pocket-watch, for example, or a set of shirt-studs. It isn't only women that go to pawnbrokers, you know.'

'In that case I'll give it to you for Christmas,' Mrs Bixby said magnanimously. 'I'll be delighted. But if it's a woman's thing, I want it myself. Is that agreed?'

'That sounds very fair. Why don't you come with me when I collect it?'

Mrs Bixby was about to say yes to this, but caught herself just in time. She had no wish to be greeted like an old customer by the pawnbroker in her husband's presence.

'No,' she said slowly. 'I don't think I will. You see, it'll be even more thrilling if I stay behind and wait. Oh, I do hope it isn't going to be something that neither of us wants.'

'You've got a point there,' he said. 'If I don't think it's worth fifty dollars, I won't even take it.'

'But you said it would be worth five hundred.'

'I'm quite sure it will. Don't worry.'

'Oh, Cyril, I can hardly wait! Isn't it exciting?'

'It's amusing,' he said, slipping the ticket into his waistcoat pocket. 'There's no doubt about that.'

Monday morning came at last, and after breakfast Mrs Bixby followed her husband to the door and helped him on with his coat.

'Don't work too hard, darling,' she said.

'No, all right.'

'Home at six?'

'I hope so.'

'Are you going to have time to go to that pawnbroker?' she asked.

'My God, I forgot all about it. I'll take a cab and go there now. It's on my way.'

'You haven't lost the ticket, have you?'

'I hope not,' he said, feeling in his waistcoat pocket. 'No, here it is.'

'And you have enough money?'

'Just about.'

'Darling,' she said, standing close to him and straightening his tie, which was perfectly straight. 'If it happens to be something nice, something you think I might like, will you telephone me as soon as you get to the office?'

'If you want me to, yes.'

'You know, I'm sort of hoping it'll be something for you, Cyril. I'd much rather it was for you than for me.'

'That's very generous of you, my dear. Now I must run.'

About an hour later, when the telephone rang, Mrs Bixby was across the room so fast she had the receiver off the hook before the first ring had finished.

'I got it!' he said.

'You did! Oh, Cyril, what was it? Was it something good?'

'Good!' he cried. 'It's fantastic! You wait till you get your eyes on this! You'll swoon!'

'Darling, what is it? Tell me quick!'

'You're a lucky girl, that's what you are.'

'It's for me, then?'

'Of course it's for you. Though how in the world it ever got to be pawned for only fifty dollars I'll be damned if I know. Someone's crazy.'

'Cyril! Stop keeping me in suspense! I can't bear it!'

'You'll go mad when you see it.'

'What is it?'

'Try to guess.'

Mrs Bixby paused. Be careful, she told herself. Be very careful now.

'A necklace,' she said.

'Wrong.'

'A diamond ring.'

'You're not even warm. I'll give you a hint. It's something you can wear.'

'Something I can wear? You mean like a hat?'

'No, it's not a hat,' he said, laughing.

'For goodness sake, Cyril! Why don't you tell me?'

'Because I want it to be a surprise. I'll bring it home with me this evening.'

'You'll do nothing of the sort!' she cried. 'I'm coming right down there to get it now!'

118

'I'd rather you didn't do that.'

'Don't be so silly, darling. Why shouldn't I come?'

'Because I'm too busy. You'll disorganise my whole morning schedule. I'm half an hour behind already.'

'Then I'll come in the lunch hour. All right?'

'I'm not having a lunch hour. Oh well, come at one-thirty then, while I'm having a sandwich. Good-bye.'

At half past one precisely, Mrs Bixby arrived at Mr Bixby's place of business and rang the bell. Her husband, in his white dentist's coat, opened the door himself.

'Oh, Cyril, I'm so excited!'

'So you should be. You're a lucky girl, did you know that?' He led her down the passage and into the surgery.

'Go and have your lunch, Miss Pulteney,' he said to the assistant, who was busy putting instruments into the steriliser. 'You can finish that when you come back.' He waited until the girl had gone, then he walked over to a closet that he used for hanging up his clothes and stood in front of it, pointing with his finger. 'It's in there,' he said. 'Now – shut your eyes.'

Mrs Bixby did as she was told. Then she took a deep breath and held it, and in the silence that followed she could hear him opening the cupboard door and there was a soft swishing sound as he pulled out a garment from among the other things hanging there.

'All right! You can look!'

'I don't dare to,' she said, laughing.

'Go on. Take a peek.'

Coyly, beginning to giggle, she raised one eyelid a fraction of an inch, just enough to give her a dark blurry view of the man standing there in his white overalls holding something up in the air.

'Mink!' he cried. 'Real mink!'

At the sound of the magic word she opened her eyes quick,

and at the same time she actually started forward in order to clasp the coat in her arms.

But there was no coat. There was only a ridiculous little fur neckpiece dangling from her husband's hand.

'Feast your eyes on that!' he said, waving it in front of her face.

Mrs Bixby put a hand up to her mouth and started backing away. I'm going to scream, she told herself. I just know it. I'm going to scream.

'What's the matter, my dear? Don't you like it?' He stopped waving the fur and stood staring at her, waiting for her to say something.

'Why yes,' she stammered. 'I … I … think it's … it's lovely … really lovely.'

'Quite took your breath away for a moment there, didn't it?'

'Yes, it did.'

'Magnificent quality,' he said. 'Fine colour, too. You know something, my dear? I reckon a piece like this would cost you two or three hundred dollars at least if you had to buy it in a shop.'

'I don't doubt it.'

There were two skins, two narrow mangy-looking skins with their heads still on them and glass beads in their eye sockets and little paws hanging down. One of them had the rear end of the other in its mouth, biting it.

'Here,' he said. 'Try it on.' He leaned forward and draped the thing around her neck, then stepped back to admire. 'It's perfect. It really suits you. It isn't everyone who has mink, my dear.'

'No, it isn't.'

'Better leave it behind when you go shopping or they'll all think we're millionaires and start charging us double.'

'I'll try to remember that, Cyril.'

'I'm afraid you mustn't expect anything else for Christmas.

120

Fifty dollars was rather more than I was going to spend anyway.'

He turned away and went over to the basin and began washing his hands. 'Run along now, my dear, and buy yourself a nice lunch. I'd take you out myself but I've got old man Gorman in the waiting-room with a broken clasp on his denture.'

Mrs Bixby moved towards the door.

I'm going to kill that pawnbroker, she told herself. I'm going right back there to the shop this very minute and I'm going to throw this filthy neckpiece right in his face and if he refuses to give me back my coat I'm going to kill him.

'Did I tell you I was going to be late home tonight?' Cyril Bixby said, still washing his hands.

'No.'

'It'll probably be at least eight-thirty the way things look at the moment. It may even be nine.'

'Yes, all right. Good-bye.' Mrs Bixby went out, slamming the door behind her.

At that precise moment, Miss Pulteney, the secretary-assistant, came sailing past her down the corridor on her way to lunch.

'Isn't it a gorgeous day?' Miss Pulteney said as she went by, flashing a smile. There was lilt in her walk, a little whiff of perfume attending her, and she looked like a queen, just exactly like a queen in the beautiful black mink coat that the Colonel had given to Mrs Bixby.

Notes on Skin

Greed and cruelty are now established themes of these short stories. The nightmarish experiences of some of Dahl's characters can only be guessed at, as they are merely suggested and not described in detail. The central character in this story, Drioli, is the unfortunate victim of cruel circumstance and greed.

What do you think?

There is great sadness at the end of this story as we consider what fate has in store for the talented Drioli. Not only has the poor widower fallen on hard times, but he carries a valuable legacy that he cannot sell. As you read, consider how Roald Dahl develops the reader's feelings for the old man, and the sense of tragedy at the end. Look at:

- the description of the old man at the beginning of the story
- his happy memories of his friend and wife
- the reasons for his falling on hard times
- the contrast between Drioli and the wealthy gallery patrons.

Questions

Look for key passages in the text that provide evidence to support your answers to these questions:

1. How do we know that Drioli is poor?

2. Describe Drioli's painter friend Chaim Soutine.

3. What is Drioli's great idea? Do you think it is a sensible one? Explain your answer.

4. What do you think really happens to Drioli at the end of the story?

Further activity

Imagine that the unfortunate Drioli's body is found. Write a newspaper report describing the events surrounding his death. You should include in your article:

- a description of the old man
- eye-witness accounts from the patrons of the art gallery who witnessed Drioli expose his painting
- an explanation of how he met his end
- you may wish to suggest who was responsible for his untimely death.

Skin

That year – 1946 – winter was a long time going. Although it was April, a freezing wind blew through the streets of the city, and overhead the snow clouds moved across the sky.

The old man who was called Drioli shuffled painfully along the sidewalk of the rue de Rivoli. He was cold and miserable, huddled up like a hedgehog in a filthy black coat, only his eyes and the top of his head visible above the turned-up collar.

The door of a café opened and the faint whiff of roasting chicken brought a pain of yearning to the top of his stomach. He moved on glancing without any interest at the things in the shop windows – perfume, silk ties and shirts, diamonds, porcelain, antique furniture, finely bound books. Then a picture gallery. He had always liked picture galleries. This one had a single canvas on display in the window. He stopped to look at it. He turned to go on. He checked, looked back; and now, suddenly, there came to him a slight uneasiness, a movement of the memory, a distant recollection of something, somewhere, he had seen before. He looked again. It was a landscape, a clump of trees leaning madly over to one side as if blown by a tremendous wind, the sky swirling and twisting all around. Attached to the frame there was a little plaque, and on this it said: CHAIM SOUTINE (1894–1943)

Drioli stared at the picture, wondering vaguely what there was about it that seemed familiar. Crazy painting, he thought. Very strange and crazy – but I like it … Chaim Soutine

Soutine … 'By God!' he cried suddenly. 'My little Kalmuck, that's who it is! My little Kalmuck with a picture in the finest shop in Paris! Just imagine that!'

The old man pressed his face closer to the window. He could remember the boy – yes, quite clearly he could remember him. But when? The rest of it was not so easy to recollect. It was so long ago. How long? Twenty – no, more like thirty years, wasn't it? Wait a minute. Yes – it was the year before the war, the first war, 1913. That was it. And this Soutine, this ugly little Kalmuck, a sullen brooding boy whom he had liked – almost loved – for no reason at all that he could think of except that he could paint.

And how he could paint! It was coming back more clearly now – the street, the line of refuse cans along the length of it, the rotten smell, the brown cats walking delicately over the refuse, and then the women, moist fat women sitting on the doorsteps with their feet upon the cobblestones of the street. Which street? Where was it the boy had lived?

The Cité Falguière, that was it! The old man nodded his head several times, pleased to have remembered the name. Then there was the studio with the single chair in it, and the filthy red couch that the boy had used for sleeping; the drunken parties, the cheap white wine, the furious quarrels, and always, always the bitter sullen face of the boy brooding over his work.

It was odd, Drioli thought, how easily it all came back to him now, how each single small remembered fact seemed instantly to remind him of another.

There was that nonsense with the tattoo, for instance. Now, that was a mad thing if ever there was one. How had it started? Ah, yes he had got rich one day, that was it, and he had bought lots of wine. He could see himself now as he entered the studio with the parcel of bottles under his arm – the boy sitting before the easel, and his (Drioli's) own wife standing in the centre of the room, posing for her picture.

'Tonight we shall celebrate,' he said. 'We shall have a little celebration, us three.'

'What is it that we celebrate?' the boy asked, without looking up. 'Is it that you have decided to divorce your wife so she can marry me?'

'No,' Drioli said. 'We celebrate because today I have made a great sum of money with my work.'

'And I have made nothing. We can celebrate that also.'

'If you like.' Drioli was standing by the table unwrapping the parcel. He felt tired and he wanted to get at the wine. Nine clients in one day was all very nice, but it could play hell with a man's eyes. He had never done as many as nine before. Nine boozy soldiers – and the remarkable thing was that no fewer than seven of them had been able to pay in cash. This had made him extremely rich. But the work was terrible on the eyes. Drioli's eyes were half closed from fatigue, the whites streaked with little connecting lines of red; and about an inch behind each eyeball there was a small concentration of pain. But it was evening now and he was wealthy as a pig, and in the parcel there were three bottles – one for his wife, one for his friend, and one for him. He had found the corkscrew and was drawing the corks from the bottles, each making a small plop as it came out.

The boy put down his brush. 'Oh, Christ,' he said. 'How can one work with all this going on?'

The girl came across the room to look at the painting. Drioli came over also, holding a bottle in one hand, a glass in the other.

'No!' the boy shouted, blazing up suddenly. 'Please – no!' He snatched the canvas from the easel and stood it against the wall. But Drioli had seen it.

'I like it.'

'It's terrible.'

'It's marvellous. Like all the others that you do, it's marvellous. I love them all.'

'The trouble is,' the boy said, scowling, 'that in themselves they are not nourishing. I cannot eat them.'

'But still they are marvellous.' Drioli handed him a tumbler full of the pale-yellow wine. 'Drink it,' he said. 'It will make you happy.'

Never, he thought, had he known a more unhappy person, or one with a gloomier face. He had spotted him in a café some seven months before, drinking alone, and because he had looked like a Russian or some sort of an Asiatic, Drioli had sat down at his table and talked.

'You are a Russian?'

'Yes.'

'Where from?'

'Minsk.'

Drioli had jumped up and embraced him, crying that he too had been born in that city.

'It wasn't actually Minsk,' the boy had said. 'But quite near.'

'Where?'

'Smilovichi, about twelve miles away.'

'Smilovichi!' Drioli had shouted, embracing him again. 'I walked there several times when I was a boy.' Then he had sat down again, staring affectionately at the other's face. 'You know,' he had said, 'you don't look like a western Russian. You're like a Tartar, or a Kalmuck. You look exactly like a Kalmuck.'

Now, standing in the studio, Drioli looked again at the boy as he took the glass of wine and tipped it down his throat in one swallow. Yes, he did have a face like a Kalmuck – very broad and high-cheeked, with a wide coarse nose. This broadness of the cheeks was accentuated by the ears which stood out sharply from the head. And then he had the narrow eyes, the black hair, the thick sullen mouth of a Kalmuck, but the hands – the hands were always a surprise, so small and white like a lady's, with tiny thin fingers.

'Give me some more,' the boy said. 'If we are to celebrate then let us do it properly.'

Drioli distributed the wine and sat himself on a chair. The boy sat on the old couch with Drioli's wife. The three bottles were placed on the floor between them.

126

'Tonight we shall drink as much as we possibly can,' Drioli said. 'I am exceptionally rich. I think perhaps I should go out now and buy some more bottles. How many shall I get?'

'Six more,' the boy said. 'Two for each.'

'Good. I shall go now and fetch them.'

'And I will help you.'

In the nearest cafe Drioli bought six bottles of white wine, and they carried them back to the studio. They placed them on the floor in two rows, and Drioli fetched the corkscrew and pulled the corks, all six of them; then they sat down again and continued to drink.

'It is only the very wealthy,' Drioli said, 'who can afford to celebrate in this manner.'

'That is true,' the boy said. 'Isn't that true, Josie?'

'Of course.'

'How do you feel, Josie?'

'Fine.'

'Will you leave Drioli and marry me?'

'No.'

'Beautiful wine,' Drioli said. 'It is a privilege to drink it.'

Slowly, methodically, they set about getting themselves drunk. The process was routine, but all the same there was a certain ceremony to be observed, and a gravity to be maintained, and a great number of things to be said, then said again – and the wine must be praised, and the slowness was important too, so that there would be time to savour the three delicious stages of transition, especially (for Drioli) the one when he began to float and his feet did not really belong to him. That was the best period of them all – when he could look down at his feet and they were so far away that he would wonder what crazy person they might belong to and why they were lying around on the floor like that, in the distance.

After a while, he got up to switch on the light. He was surprised to see that the feet came with him when he did this, especially because he couldn't feel them touching the ground. It gave him a pleasant sensation of walking on air. Then he began wandering around the room, peeking slyly at the canvases stacked against the walls.

'Listen,' he said at length. 'I have an idea.' He came across and stood before the couch, swaying gently. 'Listen, my little Kalmuck.'

'What?'

'I have a tremendous idea. Are you listening?'

'I'm listening to Josie.'

'Listen to me, *please*. You are my friend – my ugly little Kalmuck from Minsk – and to me you are such an artist that I would like to have a picture, a lovely picture – '

'Have them all. Take all you can find, but do not interrupt me when I am talking with your wife.'

'No, no. Now listen. I mean a picture that I can have with me always … for ever … wherever I go … whatever happens … but always with me … a picture by you.' He reached forward and shook the boy's knee. 'Now listen to me, *please*.'

'Listen to him,' the girl said.

'It is this. I want you to paint a picture on my skin, on my back. Then I want you to tattoo over what you have painted so that it will be there always.'

'You have crazy ideas.'

'I will teach you how to use the tattoo. It is easy. A child could do it.'

'I am not a child.'

'*Please* … '

'You are quite mad. What is it you want?' The painter looked up into the slow, dark, wine-bright eyes of the other man. 'What in heaven's name is it you want?'

'You could do it easily! You could! You could!'

'You mean with the tattoo?'

'Yes, with the tattoo! I will teach you in two minutes!'

128

'Impossible!'

'Are you saying I do not know what I am talking about?'

No, the boy could not possibly be saying that because if anyone knew about the tattoo it was he – Drioli. Had he not, only last month, covered a man's whole belly with the most wonderful and delicate design composed entirely of flowers? What about the client who had had so much hair upon his chest that he had done him a picture of a grizzly bear so designed that the hair on the chest became the furry coat of the bear? Could he not draw the likeness of a lady and position it with such subtlety upon a man's arm that when the muscle of the arm was flexed the lady came to life and performed some astonishing contortions?

'All I am saying,' the boy told him, 'is that you are drunk and this is a drunken idea.'

'We could have Josie for a model. A study of Josie upon my back. Am I not entitled to a picture of my wife upon my back?'

'Of Josie?'

'Yes.' Drioli knew he only had to mention his wife and the boy's thick brown lips would loosen and begin to quiver.

'No,' the girl said.

'Darling Josie, *please*. Take this bottle and finish it, then you will feel more generous. It is an enormous idea. Never in my life have I had such an idea before.'

'What idea?'

'That he should make a picture of you upon my back. Am I not entitled to that?'

'A picture of me?'

'A nude study,' the boy said. 'It is an agreeable idea.'

'Not nude,' the girl said.

'It is an enormous idea,' Drioli said.

'It's a damn crazy idea,' the girl said.

'It is in any event an idea,' the boy said. 'It is an idea that calls for a celebration.'

129

They emptied another bottle among them. Then the boy said, 'It is no good. I could not possibly manage the tattoo. Instead, I will paint this picture on your back and you will have it with you so long as you do not take a bath and wash it off. If you never take a bath again in your life then you will have it always, as long as you live.'

'No,' Drioli said.

'Yes – and on the day that you decide to take a bath I will know that you do not any longer value my picture. It will be a test of your admiration for my art.'

'I do not like the idea,' the girl said. 'His admiration for your art is so great that he would be unclean for many years. Let us have the tattoo. But not nude.'

'Then just the head,' Drioli said.

'I could not manage it.'

'It is immensely simple. I will undertake to teach you in two minutes. You will see. I shall go now and fetch the instruments. The needles and the inks. I have inks of many different colours – as many different colours as you have paints, and far more beautiful … '

'It is impossible.'

'I have many inks. Have I not many different colours of inks, Josie?'

'Yes.'

'You will see,' Drioli said. 'I will go now and fetch them.' He got up from his chair and walked unsteadily, but with determination, out of the room.

In half an hour Drioli was back. 'I have brought everything,' he cried, waving a brown suitcase. 'All the necessities of the tattooist are here in this bag.'

He placed the bag on the table, opened it, and laid out the electric needles and the small bottles of coloured ·inks. He plugged in the electric needle, then he took the instrument in his hand and pressed a switch. It made a buzzing sound

130

and the quarter inch of needle that projected from the end of it began to vibrate swiftly up and down. He threw off his jacket and rolled up his left sleeve. 'Now look. Watch me and I will show you how easy it is. I will make a design on my arm, here.'

His forearm was already covered with blue markings, but he selected a small clear patch of skin upon which to demonstrate.

'First, I choose my ink – let us use ordinary blue – and I dip the point of the needle in the ink … so … and I hold the needle up straight and I run it lightly over the surface of the skin … like this … and with the little motor and the electricity, the needle jumps up and down and punctures the skin and the ink goes in and there you are. See how easy it is … see how I draw a picture of a greyhound here upon my arm … '

The boy was intrigued. 'Now let *me* practise a little – on your arm.'

With the buzzing needle he began to draw blue lines upon Drioli's arm. 'It is simple,' he said. 'It is like drawing with pen and ink. There is no difference except that it is slower.'

'There is nothing to it. Are you ready? Shall we begin?'

'At once.'

'There model!' cried Drioli. 'Come on, Josie!' He was in a bustle of enthusiasm now, tottering around the room arranging everything, like a child preparing for some exciting game, 'Where will you have her? Where shall she stand?'

'Let her be standing there, by my dressing-table. Let her be brushing her hair. I will paint her with her hair down over her shoulders and her brushing it.'

'Tremendous. You are a genius.'

Reluctantly, the girl walked over and stood by the dressing table, carrying her glass of wine with her.

Drioli pulled off his shirt and stepped out of his trousers. He retained only his underpants and his socks and shoes, and he stood there swaying gently from side to side, his small body firm, white-skinned, almost hairless. 'Now,' he said, 'I am the canvas. Where will you place your canvas?'

'As always, upon the easel.'

'Don't be crazy. I am the canvas.'

'Then place yourself upon the easel. That is where you belong.'

'How can I?'

'Are you the canvas or are you not the canvas?'

'I am the canvas. Already I begin to feel like a canvas.'

'Then place yourself upon the easel. There should be no difficulty.'

'Truly, it is not possible.'

'Then sit on the chair. Sit back to front, then you can lean your drunken head against the back of it. Hurry now, for I am about to commence.'

'I am ready. I am waiting.'

'First,' the boy said, 'I shall make an ordinary painting. Then, if it pleases me, I shall tattoo over it.' With a wide brush he began to paint upon the naked skin of the man's back.

'Ayee! Ayee!' Drioli screamed. 'A monstrous centipede is marching down my spine!'

'Be still now! Be still!' The boy worked rapidly, applying the paint only in a thin blue wash so that it would not afterwards interfere with the process of tattooing. His concentration, as soon as he began to paint, was so great that it appeared somehow to supersede his drunkenness. He applied the brush strokes with quick short jabs of the arm, holding the wrist stiff, and in less than half an hour it was finished.

'All right. That's all,' he said to the girl, who immediately returned to the couch, lay down, and fell asleep.

Drioli remained awake. He watched the boy take up the needle and dip it in the ink; then he felt the sharp ticking sting as it touched the skin of his back. The pain, which was unpleasant but never extreme, kept him from going to sleep. By following the track of the needle and by watching the different colours of ink that the boy was using, Drioli amused himself trying to visualise what was going on behind him. The boy worked with an astonishing intensity. He appeared to have become completely absorbed in the little machine and in the unusual effects it was able to produce.

Far into the small hours of the morning the machine buzzed and the boy worked. Drioli could remember that when the artist finally stepped back and said, 'It is finished,' there was daylight outside and the sound of people walking in the street.

'I want to see it,' Drioli said. The boy held up a mirror, at an angle, and Drioli craned his neck to look.

'Good God!' he cried. It was a startling sight. The whole of his back, from the top of the shoulders to the base of the spine, was a blaze of colour – gold and green and blue and black and scarlet. The tattoo was applied so heavily it looked almost like an impasto. The boy had followed as closely as possible the original brush strokes, filling them in solid, and it was marvellous the way he had made use of the spine and the protrusion of the shoulder blades so that they became part of the composition. What is more, he had somehow managed to achieve – even with this slow process – a certain spontaneity. The portrait was quite alive; it contained much of that twisted, tortured quality so characteristic of Soutine's other work. It was not a good likeness. It was a mood rather than likeness, the model's face vague and tipsy, the background swirling around her head in a mass of dark-green curling strokes.

'It's tremendous!'

'I rather like it myself.' The boy stood back, examining it critically. 'You know,' he added, 'I think it's good enough for me to sign.' And taking up the buzzer again, he inscribed his name in red ink on the right-hand side, over the place where Drioli's kidney was.

133

The old man who was called Drioli was standing in a sort of trance, staring at the painting in the window of the picture-dealer's shop. It had been so long ago, all that – almost as though it had happened in another life.

And the boy? What had become of him? He could remember now that after returning from the war – the first war – he had missed him and had questioned Josie.

'Where is my little Kalmuck?'

'He is gone,' she had answered. 'I do not know where, but I heard it said that a dealer had taken him up and sent him away to Céret to make more paintings.'

'Perhaps he will return.'

'Perhaps he will. Who knows?'

That was the last time they had mentioned him. Shortly afterwards they had moved to Le Havre where there were more sailors and business was better. The old man smiled as he remembered Le Havre. Those were the pleasant years, the years between the wars, with the small shop near the docks and the comfortable rooms and always enough work, with every day three, four, five sailors coming and wanting pictures on their arms. Those were truly the pleasant years.

Then had come the second war, and Josie being killed, and the Germans arriving, and that was the finish of his business. No one had wanted pictures on their arms any more after that. And by that time he was too old for any other kind of work. In desperation he had made his way back to Paris, hoping vaguely that things would be easier in the big city. But they were not.

And now, after the war was over, he possessed neither the means nor the energy to start up his small business again. It wasn't very easy for an old man to know what to do, especially when one did not like to beg. Yet how else could he keep alive?

Well, he thought, still staring at the picture. So that is my little Kalmuck. And how quickly the sight of one small object such as this can stir the memory. Up to a few moments ago he had even forgotten that he had a tattoo on his back. It had been ages since he had thought about it. He put his face closer to the window and looked into the gallery. On the walls he could see many other pictures and all seemed to be the work of the same artist. There were a great number of people strolling around. Obviously it was a special exhibition.

On a sudden impulse, Drioli turned, pushed open the door of the gallery and went in.

It was a long room with a thick wine-coloured carpet, and by God how beautiful and warm it was. There were all these people strolling about looking at the pictures, well-washed dignified people, each of whom held a catalogue in the hand. Drioli stood just inside the door, nervously glancing around, wondering whether he dared go forward and mingle with this crowd. But before he had had time to gather his courage, he heard a voice beside him saying. 'What is it you want?'

The speaker wore a black morning coat. He was plump and short and had a very white face. It was a flabby face with so much flesh upon it that the cheeks hung down on either side of the mouth in two fleshy collops, spanielwise. He came up close to Drioli and said again, 'What is it you want?'

Drioli stood still.

'If you please,' the man was saying, 'take yourself out of my gallery.'

'Am I not permitted to look at the pictures?'

'I have asked you to leave.'

Drioli stood his ground. He felt suddenly, overwhelmingly outraged.

'Let us not have trouble,' the man was saying. 'Come on now, this way.' He put a fat white paw on Drioli's arm and began to push him firmly to the door.

That did it. 'Take your goddam hands off me!' Drioli shouted. His voice rang clear down the long gallery and all the heads jerked around as one – all the startled faces stared down the length of the room at the person who had made this noise. A flunkey came running over to help, and the two men tried to hustle Drioli through the door. The people stood still, watching the struggle. Their faces expressed only a mild interest, and seemed to be saying. 'It's all right. There's no danger to us. It's being taken care of.'

'I, too!' Drioli was shouting. 'I too, have a picture by this painter! He was my friend and I have a picture which he gave me!'

'He's mad.'

'A lunatic. A raving lunatic.'

'Someone should call the police.'

With a rapid twist of the body Drioli suddenly jumped clear of the two men, and before anyone could stop him he was running down the gallery shouting. 'I'll show you! I'll show you! I'll show you!' He flung off his overcoat, then his jacket and shirt, and he turned so that his naked back was towards the people.

'There!' he cried, breathing quickly. 'You see? There it is!' There was a sudden absolute silence in the room, each person arrested in what he was doing, standing motionless in a kind of shocked, uneasy bewilderment. They were staring at the tattooed picture. It was still there, the colours as bright as ever, but the old man's back was thinner now, the shoulder blades protruded more sharply, and the effect, though not great, was to give the picture a curiously wrinkled, squashed appearance.

Somebody said, 'My God, but it is!'

Then came the excitement and the noise of voices as the people surged forward to crowd around the old man.

'It is unmistakable!'

'His early manner, yes?'

'It is fantastic, fantastic!'

'And look, it is signed!'

'Bend your shoulders forward, my friend, so that the picture stretches out flat.'

'Old one, when was this done?'

'In 1913,' Drioli said, without turning around. 'In the autumn of 1913.'

'Who taught Soutine to tattoo?'

'I taught him.'

'And the woman?'

'She was my wife.'

The gallery owner was pushing through the crowd towards Drioli. He was calm now, deadly serious, making a smile with his mouth. 'Monsieur,' he said. 'I will buy it.' Drioli could see the loose fat upon the face vibrating as he moved his jaw. 'I said I will buy it, Monsieur.'

'How can you buy it?' Drioli asked softly.

'I will give two hundred thousand francs for it.' The dealer's eyes were small and dark, the wings of his broad nose-base were beginning to quiver.

'Don't do it!' someone murmured in the crowd. 'It is worth twenty times as much.'

Drioli opened his mouth to speak. No words came, so he shut it; then he opened it again and said slowly. 'But how can I sell it?' He lifted his hands, let them drop loosely to his sides. 'Monsieur, how can I possibly sell it?' All the sadness in the world was in his voice.

'Yes!' they were saying in the crowd. 'How can he sell it? It is part of himself!'

'Listen,' the dealer said, coming up close. 'I will help you. I will make you rich. Together we shall make some private arrangement over this picture, no?'

Drioli watched him with slow, apprehensive eyes. 'But how can you buy it, Monsieur? What will you do with it when you have bought it? Where will you keep it? Where will you keep it tonight? And where tomorrow?'

'Ah, where will I keep it? Yes, where will I keep it? Now, where will I keep it? Well, now … ' The dealer stroked the bridge of his nose with a fat white finger. 'It would seem,' he said, 'that if I take the picture, I take you also. That is a disadvantage.' He paused and stroked his nose again. 'The picture itself is of no value until you are dead. How old are you, my friend?'

'Sixty-one.'

'But you are perhaps not very robust, no?' The dealer lowered the hand from his nose and looked Drioli up and down, slowly, like a farmer appraising an old horse.

'I do not like this,' Drioli said, edging away. 'Quite honestly, Monsieur, I do not like it.' He edged straight into the arms of a tall man who put out his hands and caught him gently by the shoulders. Drioli glanced around and apologised. The man smiled down at him, patting one of the old fellow's naked shoulders reassuringly with a hand encased in a canary-coloured glove.

'Listen, my friend,' the stranger said, still smiling. 'Do you like to swim and to bask yourself in the sun?'

Drioli looked up at him, rather startled.

'Do you like fine food and red wine from the great châteaux of Bordeaux?' The man was still smiling, showing strong white teeth with a flash of gold among them. He spoke in a soft coaxing manner, one gloved hand still resting on Drioli's shoulder. 'Do you like such things?'

'Well yes,' Drioli answered, still greatly perplexed. 'Of course.'

'And the company of beautiful women?'

'Why not?'

'And a cupboard full of suits and shirts made to your own personal measurements? It would seem that you are a little lacking for clothes.'

Drioli watched this suave man, waiting for the rest of the proposition.

'Have you ever had a shoe constructed especially for your own foot?'

'You would like that?'

'Well … '

'And a man who will shave you in the mornings and trim your hair?'

Drioli simply stood and gaped.

'And a plump attractive girl to manicure the nails of your fingers?'

Someone in the crowd giggled.

'And a bell beside your bed to summon a maid to bring your breakfast in the morning? Would you like these things, my friend? Do they appeal to you?'

Drioli stood still and looked at him.

'You see, I am the owner of the Hotel Bristol in Cannes. I now invite you to come down there and live as my guest for the rest of your life in luxury and comfort.' The man paused, allowing his listener time to savour this cheerful prospect.

'Your only duty – shall I call it your pleasure, will be to spend your time on my beach in bathing trunks, walking among my guests, sunning yourself, swimming, drinking cocktails. You would like that?'

There was no answer.

'Don't you see – all the guests will thus be able to observe this fascinating picture by Soutine. You will become famous, and men will say, "Look, there is the fellow with ten million francs upon his back." You like this idea, Monsieur? It pleases you?'

Drioli looked up at the tall man in the canary gloves, still wondering whether this was some sort of a joke. 'It is a comical idea,' he said slowly. 'But do you really mean it?'

'Of course I mean it.'

'Wait,' the dealer interrupted. 'See here, old one. Here is the answer to our problem. I will buy the picture, and I will arrange with a surgeon to remove the skin from your back, and then you will be able to go off on your own and enjoy the great sum of money I shall give you for it.'

'With no skin on my back?'

'No, no, please! You misunderstand. This surgeon will put a new piece of skin in the place of the old one. It is simple.'

'Could he do that?'

'There is nothing to it.'

'Impossible!' said the man with the canary gloves. 'He's too old for such a major skin-grafting operation. It would kill him. It would kill you, my friend.'

'It would kill me?'

'Naturally. You would never survive. Only the picture would come through.'

'In the name of God!' Drioli cried. He looked around aghast at the faces of the people watching him, and in the silence that followed, another man's voice, speaking quietly from the back of the group, could be heard saying, 'Perhaps, if one were to offer this old man enough money, he might consent to kill himself on the spot. Who knows?' A few people sniggered. The dealer moved his feet uneasily on the carpet.

Then the hand in the canary glove was tapping Drioli again upon the shoulder. 'Come on,' the man was saying, smiling his broad white smile. 'You and I will go and have a good dinner and we can talk about it some more while we eat. How's that? Are you hungry?'

Drioli watched him, frowning. He didn't like the man's long flexible neck, or the way he craned it forward at you when he spoke, like a snake.

'Roast duck and Chambertin,' the man was saying. He put a rich succulent accent on the words, splashing them out with his tongue. 'And perhaps a soufflé aux marrons, light and frothy.'

Drioli's eyes turned up towards the ceiling, his lips became loose and wet. One could see the poor old fellow beginning literally to drool at the mouth.

'How do you like your duck?' the man went on. 'Do you like it very brown and crisp outside, or shall it be … '

'I am coming,' Drioli said quickly. Already he had picked up his shirt and was pulling it frantically over his head. 'Wait for me, Monsieur. I am coming.' And within a minute he had disappeared out of the gallery with his new patron.

It wasn't more than a few weeks later that a picture by Soutine, of a woman's head, painted in an unusual manner, nicely framed and heavily varnished, turned up for sale in Buenos Aires. That – and the fact that there is no hotel in Cannes called Bristol – causes one to wonder a little, and to pray for the old man's health, and to hope fervently that wherever he may be at this moment, there is a plump attractive girl to manicure the nails of his fingers, and a maid to bring him his breakfast in bed in the morning.

Notes on The Ratcatcher

Writers are often concerned with portraying unusual people who have strange and distinct characteristics. Occasionally characters bear an uncanny resemblance to a particular animal, possessing its associated behaviour and physical features. The ratcatcher of this story has obviously acquired not just the appearance of his rodent victims, but some of their more grotesque manners.

What do you think?
Traditionally rats have been portrayed as dangerous and secretive creatures with a reputation for disgusting behaviour. The repulsive nature of the ratcatcher is gradually reinforced as the story progresses. Consider how his behaviour offends Claud and the narrator. Look at:
- the ratcatcher's appearance
- his mannerisms and speech
- his rat killing techniques.

Questions
Look for words and phrases in the story that support your answers to these questions:
1. What are your first impressions of the ratcatcher? In what ways does he remind you of a rat?
2. Why do you think the ratcatcher wants to perform his tricks?
3. What is rat's blood used for, according to the ratcatcher?
4. How do Claud and the narrator react to the ratcatcher's last two methods for killing rats?

Further activity
Rewrite the story from the ratcatcher's point of view. Include the following:
- the ratcatcher's opinions of Claud and the narrator
- how the ratcatcher feels about not catching any rats at the filling station
- his reasons for demonstrating his cruel methods
- an explanation of why the ratcatcher enjoys his job so much.

The Ratcatcher

In the afternoon the ratcatcher came to the filling station. He came sidling up the driveway with a stealthy, soft-treading gait, making no noise at all with his feet on the gravel. He had an army knapsack slung over one shoulder and he was wearing an old-fashioned black jacket with large pockets. His brown corduroy trousers were tied around the knees with pieces of white string.

'Yes?' Claud asked, knowing very well who he was.

'Rodent operative.' His small dark eyes moved swiftly over the premises.

'The ratcatcher?'

'That's me.'

The man was lean and brown with a sharp face and two long sulphur-coloured teeth that protruded from the upper jaw, overlapping the lower lip, pressing it inward. The ears were thin and pointed and set far back on the head, near the nape of the neck. The eyes were almost black, but when they looked at you there was a flash of yellow somewhere inside them.

'You've come very quick.'

'Special orders from the Health Officer.'

'And now you're going to catch all the rats?'

'Yep.'

The kind of dark furtive eyes he had were those of an animal that lives its life peering out cautiously and forever from a hole in the ground.

'How are you going to catch 'em?'

'Ah-h-h,' the ratman said darkly. 'That's all accordin' to where they is.'

'Trap 'em, I suppose.'

'Trap 'em!' he cried, disgusted. 'You won't catch many rats that way! Rats isn't rabbits, you know.'

He held his face up high, sniffing the air with a nose, that twitched perceptibly from side to side.

'No,' he said, scornfully. 'Trappin's no way to catch a rat. Rats is clever, let me tell you that. If you want to catch 'em, you got to know 'em. You got to know rats on this job.'

I could see Claud staring at him with a certain fascination.

'They're more clever'n dogs, rats is.'

'Get away.'

'You know what they do? They watch you! All the time you're goin' round preparin' to catch 'em, they're sittin' quietly in dark places, watchin' you.' The man crouched, stretching his stringy neck far forward.

'So what do you do?' Claud asked, fascinated.

'Ah! That's it, you see. That's where you got to know rats.'

'How d'you catch 'em?'

'There's ways,' the ratman said, leering. 'There's various ways.'

He paused, nodding his repulsive head sagely up and down. 'It's all dependin',' he said, 'on where they is. This ain't a sewer job, is it?'

'No, it's not a sewer job.'

'Tricky things, sewer jobs. Yes,' he said, delicately sniffing the air to the left of him with his mobile nose-end, 'sewer jobs is very tricky things.'

'Not especially, I shouldn't think.'

'Oh-ho. You shouldn't, shouldn't you! Well, I'd like to see *you* do a sewer job! Just exactly how would *you* set about it, I'd like to know?'

'Nothing to it. I'd just poison 'em, that's all.'

'And where exactly would you put the poison, might I ask?'

'Down the sewer. Where the hell you think I put it!'

'There!' the ratman cried, triumphant. 'I knew it! Down the sewer! And you know what'd happen then? Get washed away, that's all. Sewer's like a river, y'know.'

'That's what you say,' Claud answered. 'That's only what *you* say.'

'It's facts.'

'All right, then, all right. So what would you do, Mr Know-all?'

'That's exactly where you got to know rats, on a sewer job.'

'Come on then, let's have it.'

'Now listen. I'll tell you.' The ratman advanced a step closer, his voice became secretive and confidential, the voice of a man divulging fabulous professional secrets. 'You works on the understandin' that a rat is a gnawin' animal, see. Rats *gnaws*. Anythin' you give 'em, don't matter what it is, anything new they never seen before, and what do they do? They *gnaws* it. So now! There are you! You get a sewer job on your hands. And what d'you do?'

His voice had the soft throaty sound of a croaking frog and he seemed to speak all his words with an immense wet-lipped relish, as though they tasted good on the tongue. The accent was similar to Claud's, the broad soft accent of the Buckinghamshire countryside, but his voice was more throaty, the words more fruity in his mouth.

'All you do is you go down the sewer and you take along some ordinary paper bags, just ordinary brown paper bags, and these bags is filled with plaster of Paris powder. Nothin' else. Then you suspend the bags from the roof of the sewer so they hang down not quite touchin' the water. See? Not quite touchin', and just high enough so a rat can reach 'em.'

Claud was listening, rapt.

'There you are, y'see. Old rat comes swimmin' along the sewer and sees the bag. He stops. He takes a sniff at it and it don't smell so bad anyway. So what's he do then?'

'He *gnaws* it,' Claud cried, delighted.

'There! That's it! That's exactly it! He starts *gnawin'* away at

145

the bag and the bag breaks and the old rat gets a mouthful of powder for his pains.'

'Well?'

'That does him.'

'What? Kills him?'

'Yep. Kills him stony!'

'Plaster of Paris ain't poisonous, you know.'

'Ah! There you are! That's exackly where you're wrong, see. This powder swells. When you wet it, it swells. Gets into the rat's tubes and swells right up and kills him quicker'n anythin' in the world.'

'*No*!'

'That's where you got to know rats.'

The ratman's face glowed with a stealthy pride, and he rubbed his stringy fingers together, holding the hands up close to the face. Claud watched him, fascinated.

'Now where's them rats?' The word 'rats' came out of his mouth soft and throaty, with a rich fruity relish as though he were gargling with melted butter. 'Let's take a look at them *rraats*.'

'Over there in the hayrick across the road.'

'Not in the house?' he asked, obviously disappointed.

'No. Only around the hayrick. Nowhere else.'

'I'll wager they're in the house too. Like as not gettin' in all your food in the night and spreadin' disease and sickness. You got any disease here?' he asked, looking first at me, then at Claud.

'Everyone's fine here.'

'Quite sure?'

'Oh yes.'

'You never know, you see. You could be sickenin' for it weeks and weeks and not feel it. Then all of a sudden bang! – and it's got you. That's why Dr Arbuthnot's so particular. That's why he sent me out so quick, see. To stop the spreadin' of disease.'

He had now taken upon himself the mantle of the Health Officer. A most important rat he was now, deeply disappointed that we were not suffering from bubonic plague.

'I feel fine,' Claud said, nervously.

The ratman searched his face again, but said nothing.

'And how are you goin' to catch 'em in the hayrick?'

The ratman grinned, a crafty toothy grin. He reached down into his knapsack and withdrew a large tin which he held up level with his face. He peered around one side of it at Claud.

'Poison!' he whispered. But he pronounced it *pye-zn*, making it into a soft, dark, dangerous word, 'Deadly *pye-zn*, that's what this is!' He was weighing the tin up and down in his hands as he spoke. 'Enough here to kill a million men!'

'Terrifying,' Claud said.

'Exackly it! They'd put you inside for six months if they caught you with even a spoonful of this,' he said, wetting his lips with his tongue. He had a habit of craning his head forward on his neck as he spoke.

'Want to see?' he asked, taking a penny from his pocket, prising open the lid. 'There now! There it is!' He spoke fondly, almost lovingly of the stuff, and he held it forward for Claud to look.

'Corn? Or barley is it?'

'It's oats. Soaked in deadly *pye-zn*. You take just one of them grains in your mouth and you'd be a gonner in five minutes.'

'Honest?'

'Yep. Never out of me sight, this tin.'

He caressed it with his hands and gave it a little shake so that the oat grains rustled softly inside.

'But not today. Your rats don't get this today. They wouldn't have it anyway. That they wouldn't. There's where you got to know rats. Rats is suspicious. Terrible suspicious, rats is. So today they gets some nice clean tasty oats as'll do 'em no harm in the world. Fatten 'em, that's all it'll do. And tomorrow they gets the same again. And it'll taste so good there'll be all the rats in the districk comin' along after a couple of days.'

'Rather clever.'

'You got to be clever on this job. You got to be cleverer'n a rat and that's sayin' something.'

'You've almost got to be a rat yourself,' I said. It slipped out in error, before I had time to stop myself, and I couldn't really help it because I was looking at the man at the time. But the effect upon him was surprising.

'There!' he cried. 'Now you got it! Now you really said something! A good ratter's got to be more like a rat than anythin' else in the world! Cleverer even than a rat, and that's not an easy thing to be, let me tell you!'

'Quite sure it's not.'

'All right, then, let's go. I haven't got all day, you know. There's Lady Leonora Benson asking for me urgent up there at the Manor.'

'She got rats, too?'

'Everybody's got rats,' the ratman said, and he ambled off down the driveway, across the road to the hayrick and we watched him go. The way he walked was so like a rat it made you wonder – that slow, almost delicate ambling walk with a lot of give at the knees and no sound at all from the footsteps on the gravel. He hopped nimbly over the gate into the field, then walked quickly round the hayrick scattering handfuls of oats on to the ground.

The next day he returned and repeated the procedure.

The day after that he came again and this time he put down the poisoned oats. But he didn't scatter these; he placed them carefully in little piles at each corner of the rick.

'You got a dog?' he asked when he came back across the road on the third day after putting down the poison.

'Yes.'

'Now if you want to see your dog die an 'orrible twistin' death, all you got to do is let him in that gate some time.'

'We'll take care,' Claud told him. 'Don't you worry about that.'

The next day he returned once more, this time to collect the dead.

'You got an old sack?' he asked. 'Most likely we goin' to need a sack to put 'em in.'

He was puffed up and important now, the black eyes gleaming with pride. He was about to display the sensational results of his craft to the audience.

Claud fetched a sack and the three of us walked across the road, the ratman leading. Claud and I leaned over the gate, watching. The ratman prowled around the hayrick, bending over to inspect his little piles of poison.

'Somethin' wrong here,' he muttered. His voice was soft and angry.

He ambled over to another pile and got down on his knees to examine it closely.

'Somethin' bloody wrong here.'

'What's the matter?'

He didn't answer, but it was clear that the rats hadn't touched his bait.

'These are very clever rats here,' I said.

'Exactly what I told him, Gordon. These aren't just no ordinary kind of rats you're dealing with here.'

The ratman walked over to the gate. He was very annoyed and showed it on his face and around the nose and by the way the two yellow teeth were pressing down into the skin of his lower lip. 'Don't give me that crap,' he said, looking at me. 'There's nothin' wrong with these rats except somebody's feedin' 'em. They got somethin' juicy to eat somewhere and plenty of it. There's no rats in the world'll turn down oats unless their bellies is full to burstin'.'

'They're clever,' Claud said.

The man turned away, disgusted. He knelt down again and began to scoop up the poisoned oats with a small shovel, tipping them carefully back into the tin. When he had done, all three of us walked back across the road.

The ratman stood near the petrol-pumps, a rather sorry, humble ratman now whose face was beginning to take on a brooding aspect. He had withdrawn into himself and was brooding silence over his failure, the eyes veiled and wicked, the little tongue darting out to one side of the two yellow teeth, keeping the lips moist. It appeared to be essential that the lips should be kept moist. He looked up at me, a quick surreptitious glance, then over at Claud. His nose-end twitched, sniffing the air. He raised himself up and down a few times on his toes, swaying gently, and in a voice soft and secretive, he said: 'Want to see somethin'?' He was obviously trying to retrieve his reputation.

'What?'

'Want to see somethin' *amazin'*?' As he said this he put his right hand into the deep poacher's pocket of his jacket and brought out a large live rat clasped tight between his fingers.

'Good God!'

'Ah! That's it, y'see!' He was crouching slightly now and craning his neck forward and leering at us and holding this enormous brown rat in his hands, one finger and thumb making a tight circle around the creature's neck, clamping its head rigid so it couldn't turn and bite.

'D'you usually carry rats around in your pockets?'

'Always got a rat or two about me somewhere.'

With that he put his free hand into the other pocket and produced a small white ferret.

'Ferret,' he said, holding it up by the neck.

The ferret seemed to know him and stayed still in his grasp.

'There's nothin'll kill a rat quicker'n a ferret. And there's nothin' a rat's more frightened of either.'

He brought his hands close together in front of him so that the ferret's nose was within six inches of the rat's face. The pink beady eyes of the ferret stared at the rat. The rat struggled, trying to edge away from the killer.

'Now,' he said. 'Watch'.

His khaki shirt was open at the neck and he lifted the rat and slipped it down inside his shirt, next to his skin. As soon as his hand was free, he unbuttoned his jacket at the front so that the audience could see the bulge the body of the rat made under his shirt. His belt prevented it from going down lower than his waist.

Then he slipped the ferret in after the rat.

Immediately there was a great commotion inside the shirt. It appeared that the rat was running around the man's body, being chased by the ferret. Six or seven times they went around, the small bulge chasing the larger one, gaining on it slightly each circuit and drawing closer and closer until at last the two bulges seemed to come together and there was a scuffle and a series of shrill shrieks.

Throughout this performance the ratman had stood absolutely still with legs apart, arms hanging loosely, the dark eyes resting on Claud's face. Now he reached one hand down into his shirt and pulled out the ferret; with the other he took out the dead rat. There were traces of blood around the white muzzle of the ferret.

'Not sure I liked that very much.'

'You never seen anything' like it before, I'll bet you that.'

'Can't really say I have.'

'Like as not you'll get yourself a nasty little nip in the guts one of these days,' Claud told him. But he was clearly impressed, and the ratman was becoming cocky again.

'Want to see somethin' far more *amazn'n* that?' he asked. 'You want to see somethin' you'd never even *believe* unless you seen it with your own eyes?'

'Well?'

We were standing in the driveway out in front of the pumps and it was one of those pleasant warm November mornings. Two cars pulled in for petrol, one right after the other, and Claud went over and gave them what they wanted.

'You want to see?' the ratman asked.

I glanced at Claud, slightly apprehensive. 'Yes,' Claud said. 'Come on then, let's see.'

The ratman slipped the dead rat back into one pocket, the ferret into the other. Then he reached down into his knapsack and produced – if you please – a second live rat.

'Good Christ!' Claud said.

'Always got one or two rats about me somewhere,' the man announced calmly. 'You got to know rats on this job, and if you want to know 'em you got to have 'em round you. This is a sewer rat, this is. An old sewer rat, clever as buggery. See him watchin' me all the time, wonderin' what I'm goin' to do? See him?'

'Very unpleasant.'

'What are you going to do?' I asked. I had a feeling I was going to like this one even less than the last.

'Fetch me a piece of string.'

Claud fetched him a piece of string.

With his left hand, the man looped the string around one of the rat's hind legs. The rat struggled, trying to turn its head to see what was going on, but he held it tight around the neck with finger and thumb.

'Now!' he said, looking about him. 'You got a table inside?'

'We don't want the rat inside the house,' I said.

'Well – I need a table. Or somethin' flat like a table.'

'What about the bonnet of that car?' Claud said.

We walked over to the car and the man put the old sewer rat on the bonnet. He attached the string to the windshield wiper so that the rat was now tethered.

At first it crouched, unmoving and suspicious, a big-bodied grey rat with bright black eyes and a scaly tail that lay in a long curl upon the car's bonnet. It was looking away from the ratman, but watching him sideways to see what he was going to do. The man stepped back a few paces and immediately the rat relaxed. It sat up on its haunches and began to lick the grey fur on its chest. Then it scratched its muzzle with both front paws. It seemed quite unconcerned about the three men standing near by.

'Now – how about a little bet?' the ratman asked.

'We don't bet,' I said.

'Just for fun. It's more fun if you bet.'

'What d'you want to bet on?'

'I'll bet you I can kill that rat without usin' my hands. I'll put my hands in my pockets and not use 'em.'

'You'll kick it with your feet,' Claud said.

It was apparent that the ratman was out to earn some money. I looked at the rat that was going to be killed and began to feel slightly sick, not so much because it was going to be killed but because it was going to be killed in a special way, with a considerable degree of relish.

'No,' the ratman said. 'No feet.'

'Nor arms?' Claud asked.

'Nor arms. Nor legs, nor hands neither.'

'You'll sit on it.'

'No. No squashin'.'

'Let's see you do it.'

'You bet me first. Bet me a quid.'

'Don't be so bloody daft,' Claud said. 'Why should we give you a quid?'

'What'll you bet?'

153

'Nothin'.'

'All right. Then it's no go.'

He made as if to untie the string from the windshield wiper.

'I'll bet you a shilling,' Claud told him. The sick gastric sensation in my stomach was increasing, but there was an awful magnetism about this business and I found myself quite unable to walk away or even move.

'You too?'

'No,' I said.

'What's the matter with you?' the ratman asked.

'I just don't want to bet you, that's all.'

'So you want me to do this for a lousy shillin'?'

'I don't want you to do it.'

'Where's the money?' he said to Claud.

Claud put a shilling piece on the bonnet, near the radiator. The ratman produced two sixpences and laid them beside Claud's money. As he stretched out his hand to do this, the rat cringed, drawing its head back and flattening itself against the bonnet.

'Bet's on,' the ratman said.

Claud and I stepped back a few paces. The ratman stepped forward. He put his hands in his pockets and inclined his body from the waist so that his face was on a level with the rat, about three feet away.

His eyes caught the eyes of the rat and held them. The rat was crouching, very tense, sensing extreme danger, but not yet frightened. The way it crouched, it seemed to me it was preparing to spring forward at the man's face; but there must have been some power in the ratman's eyes that prevented it from doing this, and subdued it, and then gradually frightened it so that it began to back away, dragging its body backwards with slow crouching steps until the string tautened on its hind leg. It tried to struggle back further against the string, jerking its leg to free it. The man leaned forward towards the rat, following

154

it with his face, watching it all the time with his eyes, and suddenly the rat panicked and leaped sideways in the air. The string pulled it up with a jerk that must almost have dislocated its leg.

It crouched again, in the middle of the bonnet, as far away as the string would allow, and it was properly frightened now, whiskers quivering, the long grey body tense with fear.

At this point, the ratman again began to move his face closer. Very slowly he did it, so slowly there wasn't really any movement to be seen at all except that the face just happened to be a fraction closer each time you looked. He never took his eyes from the rat. The tension was considerable and I wanted suddenly to cry out and tell him to stop. I wanted him to stop because it was making me feel sick inside, but I couldn't bring myself to say the word. Something extremely unpleasant was about to happen – I was sure of that. Something sinister and cruel and ratlike, and perhaps it really would make me sick. But I had to see it now.

The ratman's face was about eighteen inches from the rat. Twelve inches. Then ten, or perhaps it was eight, and then there was not more than the length of a man's hand separating their faces. The rat was pressing its body flat against the car bonnet, tense and terrified. The ratman was also tense, but with a dangerous active tensity that was like a tight-wound spring. The shadow of a smile flickered around the skin of his mouth.

Then suddenly he struck.

He struck as a snake strikes, darting his head forward with one swift knifelike stroke that originated in the muscles of the lower body, and I had a momentary glimpse of his mouth opening very wide and two yellow teeth and the whole face contorted by the effort of mouth-opening.

More than that I did not care to see. I closed my eyes, and when I opened them again the rat was dead and the ratman was slipping the money into his pocket and spitting to clear his mouth.

'That's what they makes lickerish out of,' he said. 'Rat's blood is what the big factories and the chocolate-people use to make lickerish.'

Again the relish, the wet-lipped, lip-smacking relish as he spoke the words, the throaty richness of his voice and the thick syrupy way he pronounced the word *lickerish.*

'No.' he said, 'there's nothin' wrong with a drop of rat's blood.'

'Don't talk so absolutely disgusting,' Claud told him.

'Ah! But that's it, you see. You eaten it many a time. Penny sticks and lickerish bootlaces is all made from rat's blood.'

'We don't want to hear about it, thank you.'

'Boiled up, it is, in great cauldrons, bubblin' and steamin' and men stirrin' it with long poles. That's one of the big secrets of the chocolate-makin' factories, and no one knows about it – no one except the ratters supplyin' the stuff.'

Suddenly he noticed that his audience was no longer with him, that our faces were hostile and sick-looking and crimson with anger and disgust. He stopped abruptly, and without another word he turned and sloped off down the driveway out on to the road, moving with the slow, that almost delicate ambling walk that was like a rat prowling, making no noise with his footsteps even on the gravel of the driveway.

Notes on The Hitchhiker

Roald Dahl's fascination with danger and risk-taking is well documented. In 'The Hitchhiker' we once again witness the excitement that can be gained from unlawful or dangerous activities. His dislike and distrust of heavy-handed authority is once again in evidence. The policeman in 'The Hitchhiker' comes in for the same treatment as the incompetent gamekeepers in 'The Champion of the World'.

What do you think?

Our opinion of the hitchhiker changes as the story progresses. Initially we are suspicious of him but eventually we share the narrator's admiration for his 'trade'. Think about:

- the unpleasant characteristics displayed by the hitchhiker at the beginning of the story
- the attitude of the policeman
- the way the hitchhiker gains our admiration
- your opinion of the hitchhiker at the end of the story.

Questions

Look for words and phrases to support your answers to these questions:

1. What are your first impressions of the hitchhiker? What words and phrases in the text suggest that he is a suspicious character?
2. Why does the narrator pick up the hitchhiker?
3. How do the two occupants of the car react to the policeman? What impression of the policeman does the writer want us to form?
4. What does the hitchhiker think of pickpockets?
5. How does the writer change the reader's opinion of the hitchhiker by the end of the story? What are your final impressions of the hitchhiker?

Further activity

Imagine you are the policeman in the story. You are very annoyed when you get back to the police station and discover that both your books have disappeared. You decide to issue details of the two men to your colleagues so that they can be caught. Produce identikit pictures and written descriptions of the two occupants of the car.

The Hitchhiker

I had a new car. It was an exciting toy, a big BMW 3.3 Li, which means 3.3 litre, long wheelbase, fuel injection. It had a top speed of 129 m.p.h. and terrific acceleration. The body was pale blue. The seats inside were darker blue and they were made of leather, genuine soft leather of the finest quality. The windows were electrically operated and so was the sun-roof. The radio aerial popped up when I switched on the radio, and disappeared when I switched it off. The powerful engine growled and grunted impatiently at slow speeds, but at sixty miles an hour the growling stopped and the motor began to purr with pleasure.

I was driving up to London by myself. It was a lovely June day. They were haymaking in the fields and there were buttercups along both sides of the road. I was whispering along at seventy miles an hour, leaning back comfortably in my seat, with no more than a couple of fingers resting lightly on the wheel to keep her steady. Ahead of me I saw a man thumbing a lift. I touched the footbrake and brought the car to a stop beside him. I always stopped for hitch-hikers. I knew just how it used to feel to be standing on the side of a country road watching the cars go by. I hated the drivers for pretending they didn't see me, especially the ones in big cars with three empty seats. The large expensive cars seldom stopped. It was always the smaller ones that offered you a lift, or the old rusty ones, or the ones that were already crammed full of children and the driver would say, 'I think we can squeeze in one more.'

The hitch-hiker poked his head through the open window and said, 'Going to London, guv'nor?'

'Yes,' I said. 'Jump in.'

He got in and I drove on.

He was a small ratty-faced man with grey teeth. His eyes were dark and quick and clever, like a rat's eyes, and his ears were slightly pointed at the top. He had a cloth cap on his head and he was wearing a greyish-coloured jacket with enormous pockets. The grey jacket, together with the quick eyes and the pointed ears, made him look more than anything like some sort of a huge human rat.

'What part of London are you headed for?' I asked him.

'I'm goin' right through London and out the other side,' he said. 'I'm goin' to Epsom, for the races. It's Derby Day today.'

'So it is,' I said. 'I wish I were going with you. I love betting on horses.'

'I never bet on horses,' he said. 'I don't even watch 'em run. That's a stupid silly business.'

'Then why do you go?' I asked.

He didn't seem to like that question. His little ratty face went absolutely blank and he sat there staring straight ahead at the road, saying nothing.

'I expect you help to work the betting machines or something like that,' I said.

'That's even sillier,' he answered. 'There's no fun working them lousy machines and selling tickets to mugs. Any fool could do that.'

There was a long silence. I decided not to question him any more. I remembered how irritated I used to get in my hitch-hiking days when drivers kept asking *me* questions. Where are you going? Why are you going there? What's your job? Are you married? Do you have a girl-friend? What's her name? How old are you? And so on and so forth. I used to hate it.

'I'm sorry,' I said. 'It's none of my business what you do. The trouble is, I'm a writer, and most writers are terrible nosey parkers.'

'You write books?' he asked.

'Yes.'

'Writin' books is okay,' he said. 'It's what I call a skilled trade. I'm in a skilled trade too. The folks I despise is them that spend all their lives doin' crummy old routine jobs with no skill in 'em at all. You see what I mean?'

'Yes.'

'The secret of life,' he said, 'is to become very very good at somethin' that's very very 'ard to do.'

'Like you,' I said.

'Exactly. You and me both.'

'What makes you think that I'm any good at my job?' I asked. 'There's an awful lot of bad writers around.'

'You wouldn't be drivin' about in a car like this if you weren't no good at it,' he answered. 'It must've cost a tidy packet, this little job.'

'It wasn't cheap.'

'What can she do flat out?' he asked.

'One hundred and twenty-nine miles an hour,' I told him.

'I'll bet she won't do it.'

'I'll bet she will.'

'All car makers is liars,' he said. 'You can buy any car you like and it'll never do what the makers say it will in the ads.'

'This one will.'

'Open 'er up then and prove it,' he said. 'Go on, guv'nor, open 'er right up and let's see what she'll do.'

There is a roundabout at Chalfont St Peter and immediately beyond it there's a long straight section of dual carriage-way. We came out of the roundabout on to the carriage-way and I pressed my foot hard down on the accelerator. The big car leaped forward as though she'd been stung. In ten seconds or so, we were doing ninety.

'Lovely!' he cried. 'Beautiful! Keep goin'!'

I had the accelerator jammed right down against the floor and I held it there.

'One hundred!' he shouted … 'A hundred and five! … A

161

hundred and ten! … A hundred and fifteen! Go on! Don't slack off!'

I was in the outside lane and we flashed past several cars as though they were standing still – a green Mini, a big cream-coloured Citroen, a white Land-Rover, a huge truck with a container on the back, an orange-coloured Volkswagen Minibus …

'A hundred and twenty!' my passenger shouted, jumping up and down. 'Go on! Go on! Get 'er up to one-two-nine!'

At that moment, I heard the scream of a police siren. It was so loud it seemed to be right inside the car, and then a policeman on a motor-cycle loomed up alongside us on the inside lane and went past us and raised a hand for us to stop.

'Oh, my sainted aunt!' I said. 'That's torn it!'

The policeman must have been doing about a hundred and thirty when he passed us, and he took plenty of time slowing down. Finally, he pulled into the side of the road and I pulled in behind him. 'I didn't know police motor-cycles could go as fast as that,' I said rather lamely.

'That one can,' my passenger said. 'It's the same make as yours. It's a BMW R90S. Fastest bike on the road. That's what they're usin' nowadays.'

The policeman got off his motor-cycle and leaned the machine sideways on to its prop stand. Then he took off his gloves and placed them carefully on the seat. He was in no hurry now. He had us where he wanted us and he knew it.

'This is real trouble,' I said. 'I don't like it one bit.'

'Don't talk to 'im any more than is necessary, you understand,' my companion said. 'Just sit tight and keep mum.'

Like an executioner approaching his victim, the policeman came strolling slowly toward us. He was a big meaty man with a belly, and his blue breeches were skin-tight around his enormous thighs. His goggles were pulled up on to the helmet, showing a smouldering red face with wide cheeks.

We sat there like guilty schoolboys, waiting for him to arrive.

'Watch out for this man,' my passenger whispered. ''Ee looks mean as the devil.'

The policeman came round to my open window and placed one meaty hand on the sill. 'What's the hurry?' he said.

'No hurry, officer,' I answered.

'Perhaps there's a woman in the back having a baby and you're rushing her to hospital? Is that it?'

'No, officer.'

'Or perhaps your house is on fire and you're dashing home to rescue the family from upstairs?' His voice was dangerously soft and mocking.

'My house isn't on fire, officer.'

'In that case,' he said, 'you've got yourself into a nasty mess, haven't you? Do you know what the speed limit is in this country?'

'Seventy,' I said.

'And do you mind telling me exactly what speed you were doing just now?'

I shrugged and didn't say anything.

When he spoke next, he raised his voice so loud that I jumped. *'One hundred and twenty miles per hour!'* he barked. 'That's *fifty* miles an hour over the limit!'

He turned his head and spat out a big gob of spit. It landed on the wing of my car and started sliding down over my beautiful blue paint. Then he turned back again and stared hard at my passenger. 'And who are you?' he asked sharply.

'He's a hitch-hiker,' I said. 'I'm giving him a lift.'

'I didn't ask you,' he said. 'I asked him.'

''Ave I done somethin' wrong?' my passenger asked. His voice was as soft and oily as haircream.

'That's more than likely,' the policeman answered. 'Anyway, you're a witness. I'll deal with you in a minute. Driving-licence,' he snapped, holding out his hand.

163

I gave him my driving-licence.

He unbuttoned the left-hand breast-pocket of his tunic and brought out the dreaded book of tickets. Carefully, he copied the name and address from my licence. Then he gave it back to me. He strolled round to the front of the car and read the number from the number-plate and wrote that down as well. He filled in the date, the time and the details of my offence. Then he tore out the top copy of the ticket. But before handing it to me, he checked that all the information had come through clearly on his own carbon copy. Finally, he replaced the book in his tunic pocket and fastened the button.

'Now you,' he said to my passenger, and he walked around to the other side of the car. From the other breast-pocket he produced a small black notebook. 'Name?' he snapped.

'Michael Fish,' my passenger said.

'Address?'

'Fourteen, Windsor Lane, Luton.'

'Show me something to prove this is your real name and address,' the policeman said.

My passenger fished in his pockets and came out with a driving-licence of his own. The policeman checked the name and address and handed it back to him. 'What's your job?' he asked sharply.

'I'm an 'od carrier.'

'A *what*?'

'An 'od carrier.'

'Spell it.'

'H-O-D-C-A- ... '

'That'll do. And what's a hod carrier, may I ask?'

'An 'od carrier, officer, is a person 'oo carries the cement up the ladder to the bricklayer. And the 'od is what 'ee carries it in. It's got a long 'andle, and on the top you've got two bits of wood set at an angle.'

'All right, all right. Who's your employer?'

'Don't 'ave one. I'm unemployed.'

The policeman wrote all this down in the black notebook. Then he returned the book to its pocket and did up the button.

'When I get back to the station I'm going to do a little checking up on you,' he said to my passenger.

'Me? What've I done wrong?' the rat-faced man asked.

'I don't like your face, that's all,' the policeman said. 'And we just might have a picture of it somewhere in our files.' He strolled round the car and returned to my window.

'I suppose you know you're in serious trouble,' he said to me.

'Yes, officer.'

'You won't be driving this fancy car of yours again for a very long time, not after *we've* finished with you. You won't be driving *any* car again come to that for several years. And a good thing, too. I hope they lock you up for a spell into the bargain.'

'You mean prison?' I asked, alarmed.

'Absolutely,' he said, smacking his lips. 'In the clink. Behind the bars. Along with all the other criminals who break the law. *And* a hefty fine into the bargain. Nobody will be more pleased about that than me. I'll see you in court, both of you. You'll be getting a summons to appear.'

He turned away and walked over to his motor-cycle. He flipped the prop stand back into position with his foot and swung his leg over the saddle. Then he kicked the starter and roared off up the road out of sight.

'Phew!' I gasped. 'That's done it.'

'We was caught,' my passenger said. 'We was caught good and proper.'

'I was caught, you mean.'

'That's right,' he said. 'What you goin' to do now, guv'nor?'

'I'm going straight up to London to talk to my solicitor,' I said. I started the car and drove on.

'You mustn't believe what 'ee said to you about goin' to

165

prison,' my passenger said. 'They don't put nobody in the clink just for speedin'.'

'Are you sure of that?' I asked.

'I'm positive,' he answered. 'They can take your licence away and they can give you a whoppin' big fine, but that'll be the end of it.'

I felt tremendously relieved.

'By the way,' I said, 'why did you lie to him?'

'Who, me?' he said. 'What makes you think I lied?'

'You told him you were an unemployed hod carrier. But you told *me* you were in a highly skilled trade.'

'So I am,' he said. 'But it don't pay to tell everythin' to a copper.'

'So what *do* you do?' I asked him.

'Ah,' he said slyly. 'That'd be tellin', wouldn't it?'

'Is it something you're ashamed of?'

'Ashamed?' he cried. 'Me, ashamed of my job? I'm about as proud of it as anybody could be in the entire world!'

'Then why won't you tell me?'

'You writers really is nosey parkers, aren't you?' he said. 'And you ain't goin' to be 'appy, I don't think, until you've found out exactly what the answer is.'

'I don't really care one way or the other,' I told him, lying.

He gave me a crafty little ratty look out of the sides of his eyes. 'I think you do care,' he said. 'I can see it on your face that you think I'm in some kind of a very peculiar trade and you're just achin' to know what it is.'

I didn't like the way he read my thoughts. I kept quiet and stared at the road ahead.

'You'd be right, too,' he went on. 'I *am* in a very peculiar trade. I'm in the queerest peculiar trade of 'em all.'

I waited for him to go on.

'That's why I 'as to be extra careful 'oo I'm talking' to, you see.

'Ow am I to know, for instance, you're not another copper in plain clothes?'

'Do I look like a copper?'

'No,' he said. 'You don't. And you ain't. Any fool could tell that.'

He took from his pocket a tin of tobacco and a packet of cigarette papers and started to roll a cigarette. I was watching him out of the corner of one eye, and the speed with which he performed this rather difficult operation was incredible. The cigarette was rolled and ready in about five seconds. He ran his tongue along the edge of the paper, stuck it down and popped the cigarette between his lips. Then, as if from nowhere, a lighter appeared in his hand. The lighter flamed. The cigarette was lit. The lighter disappeared. It was altogether a remarkable performance.

'I've never seen anyone roll a cigarette as fast as that,' I said.

'Ah,' he said, taking a deep suck of smoke. 'So you noticed.'

'Of course I noticed. It was quite fantastic.'

He sat back and smiled. It pleased him very much that I had noticed how quickly he could roll a cigarette. 'You want to know what makes me able to do it?' he asked.

'Go on then.'

'It's because I've got fantastic fingers. These fingers of mine,' he said, holding up both hands high in front of him, 'are quicker and cleverer than the fingers of the best piano player in the world!'

'Are you a piano player?'

'Don't be daft,' he said. 'Do I look like a piano player?'

I glanced at his fingers. They were so beautifully shaped, so slim and long and elegant, they didn't seem to belong to the rest of him at all. They looked more like the fingers of a brain surgeon or a watchmaker.

'My job,' he went on, 'is a hundred times more difficult than playin' the piano. Any twerp can learn to do that. There's titchy little kids learnin' to play the piano in almost any 'ouse you go into these days. That's right, ain't it?'

'More or less,' I said.

'Of course it's right. But there's not one person in ten million can learn to do what I do. Not one in ten million! 'Ow about that?'

'Amazing,' I said.

'You're darn right it's amazin',' he said.

'I think I know what you do,' I said. 'You do conjuring tricks. You're a conjurer.'

'Me?' he snorted. 'A conjurer? Can you picture me goin' round crummy kids' parties makin' rabbits come out of top 'ats?'

'Then you're a card player. You get people into card games and you deal yourself marvellous hands.'

'Me! A rotten card-sharper!' he cried. 'That's a miserable racket if ever there was one.'

'All right. I give up.'

I was taking the car along slowly now, at no more than forty miles an hour, to make quite sure I wasn't stopped again. We had come on to the main London-Oxford road and were running down the hill toward Denham.

Suddenly, my passenger was holding up a black leather belt in his hand. 'Ever seen this before?' he asked. The belt had a brass buckle of unusual design.

'Hey!' I said. 'That's mine, isn't it? It *is* mine! Where did you get it?'

He grinned and waved the belt gently from side to side. 'Where d'you think I got it?' he said. 'Off the top of your trousers, of course.'

I reached down and felt for my belt. It was gone.

'You mean you took it off me while we've been driving along?' I asked, flabbergasted.

He nodded, watching me all the time with those little black ratty eyes.

'That's impossible,' I said. 'You'd have had to undo the buckle and slide the whole thing out through the loops all the way round. I'd have seen you doing it. And even if I hadn't seen you, I'd have felt it.'

'Ah, but you didn't, did you?' he said, triumphant. He dropped the belt on his lap, and now all at once there was a brown shoelace dangling from his fingers. 'And what about this, then?' he exclaimed, waving the shoelace.

'What about it?' I said.

'Anyone around 'ere missin' a shoelace?' he asked, grinning.

I glanced down at my shoes. The lace of one of them was missing. 'Good grief!' I said. 'How did you do that? I never saw you bending down.'

'You never saw nothin',' he said proudly. 'You never even saw me move an inch. And you know why?'

'Yes,' I said. 'Because you've got fantastic fingers.'

'Exactly right!' he cried. 'You catch on pretty quick, don't you?' He sat back and sucked away at his home-made cigarette, blowing the smoke out in a thin stream against the windshield. He knew he had impressed me greatly with those two tricks, and this made him very happy. 'I don't want to be late,' he said. 'What time is it?'

'There's a clock in front of you,' I told him.

'I don't trust car clocks,' he said. 'What does your watch say?'

I hitched up my sleeve to look at the watch on my wrist. It wasn't there. I looked at the man. He looked back at me grinning.

'You've taken that, too,' I said.

He held out his hand and there was my watch lying in his palm. 'Nice bit of stuff, this,' he said. 'Superior quality. Eighteen-carat gold. Easy to flog, too. It's never any trouble gettin' rid of quality goods.'

'I'd like it back, if you don't mind,' I said rather huffily.

169

He placed the watch carefully on the leather tray in front of him. 'I wouldn't nick anything from you, guv'nor,' he said. 'You're my pal. You're givin' me a lift.'

'I'm glad to hear it,' I said.

'All I'm doin' is answerin' your question,' he went on. 'You asked me what I did for a livin' and I'm showin' you.'

'What else have you got of mine?'

He smiled again, and now he started to take from the pocket of his jacket one thing after another that belonged to me – my driving-licence, a key-ring with four keys on it, some pound notes, a few coins, a letter from my publishers, my diary, a stubby old pencil, a cigarette-lighter, and last of all, a beautiful old sapphire ring with pearls around it belonging to my wife. I was taking the ring up to the jeweller in London because one of the pearls was missing.

'Now *there's* another lovely piece of goods,' he said, turning the ring over in his fingers. 'That's eighteenth century, if I'm not mistaken, from the reign of King George the Third.'

'You're right,' I said, impressed. 'You're absolutely right.'

He put the ring on the leather tray with the other items.

'So you're a pickpocket,' I said.

'I don't like that word,' he answered. 'It's a coarse and vulgar word. Pickpockets is coarse and vulgar people who only do easy little amateur jobs. They lift money from blind old ladies.'

'What do you call yourself, then?'

'Me? I'm a fingersmith. I'm a professional fingersmith.' He spoke the words solemnly and proudly, as though he were telling me he was the President of the Royal College of Surgeons or the Archbishop of Canterbury.

'I've never heard that word before,' I said. 'Did you invent it?'

'Of course I didn't invent it,' he replied. 'It's the name given to them who's risen to the very top of the profession. You've 'eard of a goldsmith and a silversmith, for instance. They're experts with gold and silver. I'm an expert with my fingers, so I'm a fingersmith.'

'It must be an interesting job.'

'It's a marvellous job,' he answered. 'It's lovely.'

'And that's why you go to the races?'

'Race meetings is easy meat,' he said. 'You just stand around after the race, watchin' for the lucky ones to queue up and draw their money. And when you see someone collectin' a big bundle of notes, you simply follows after 'im and 'elps yourself. But don't get me wrong, guv'nor. I never takes nothin' from a loser. Nor from poor people neither. I only go after them as can afford it, the winners and the rich.'

'That's very thoughtful of you,' I said. 'How often do you get caught?'

'Caught?' he cried, disgusted. '*Me* get caught! It's only pickpockets get caught. Fingersmiths never. Listen, I could take the false teeth out of your mouth if I wanted to and you wouldn't even catch me!'

'I don't have false teeth,' I said.

'I know you don't,' he answered. 'Otherwise I'd 'ave 'ad 'em out long ago!'

I believed him. Those long slim fingers of his seemed able to do anything.

We drove on for a while without talking.

'That policeman's going to check up on you pretty thoroughly,' I said. 'Doesn't that worry you a bit?'

'Nobody's checkin' up on me,' he said.

'Of course they are. He's got your name and address written down most carefully in his black book.'

The man gave me another of his sly, ratty little smiles. 'Ah,' he said. 'So 'ee 'as. But I'll bet 'ee ain't got it all written down in 'is memory as well. I've never known a copper yet with a decent memory. Some of 'em can't even remember their own names.'

'What's memory got to do with it?' I asked. 'It's written down in his book, isn't it?'

'Yes, guv'nor, it is. But the trouble is, 'ee's lost the book. 'Ee's lost both books, the one with my name in it *and* the one with yours.'

In the long delicate fingers of his right hand, the man was holding up in triumph the two books he had taken from the policeman's pockets. 'Easiest job I ever done,' he announced proudly.

I nearly swerved the car into a milk-truck, I was so excited.

'That copper's got nothing on either of us now,' he said.

'You're a genius!' I cried.

''Ee's got no names, no addresses, no car number, no nothin',' he said.

'You're brilliant!'

'I think you'd better pull in off this main road as soon as possible,' he said. 'Then we'd better build a little bonfire and burn these books.'

'You're a fantastic fellow,' I exclaimed.

'Thank you, guv'nor,' he said. 'It's always nice to be appreciated.'

Further reading

Further collections by Roald Dahl
Completely Unexpected Tales (Penguin, 1986)
Kiss, Kiss (Penguin, 1969)
More Tales of the Unexpected (Penguin, 1995)
Over to You: Ten Short Stories of Flying (Penguin, 1996)
Someone Like You (Penguin, 1970)
Switch Bitch (Penguin, 1976)
Tales of the Unexpected (Penguin, 1995)
Taste and Other Tales (Longman, 1999)
The Great Automatic Grammartizator and Other Stories (Penguin, 1997)
The Wonderful World of Henry Sugar (Penguin, 1995)

Other works by Roald Dahl
Boy (Puffin, 1995)
Charlie and the Chocolate Factory (Penguin, 1987)
Charlie and the Great Glass Elevator (Penguin, 1997)
Danny, the Champion of the World (Penguin, 1994)
Going Solo (Penguin, 1988)
James and the Giant Peach (Penguin, 1996)
Matilda (Penguin, 1996)
The BFG (Penguin, 1999)
The Giraff and the Pelly and Me (Penguin, 1993)

Programme of study

It is envisaged that each of the following tasks will help students to understand the different ways an author's choice of language and structural devices can construct meaning, develop characters and create different moods. Each task, and its related passage, is set within the context of one of the stories in this selection, thereby allowing pupils to explore the techniques used by a writer within a real context.

Word and sentence
Nouns
In this task you will look at simple concrete nouns and consider how they can be used to create a vivid picture in the mind's eye of the reader.

1. Identify at least ten concrete nouns in the following passage from 'Lamb to the Slaughter':

   The room was warm and clean, the curtains drawn, the two table lamps alight – hers and the one by the empty chair opposite. On the sideboard behind her, two tall glasses, soda water, whisky. Fresh ice cubes in the Thermos bucket.

   Mary Maloney was waiting for her husband to come home from work.

   Now and again she would glance up at the clock, but without anxiety

2. Write a description of a room in your house including as many suitable concrete nouns as you can think of.

Verbs
In this task you will look at verbs and consider how they can change and affect meaning.

3. Pick out all the verbs in the following passage from 'The Champion of the World' and explain what they mean. How does each one add interest to the description?

All day, in between serving customers, we had been crouching over the table in the office of the filling-station, preparing the raisins. They were plump and soft and swollen from being soaked in water, and when you nicked them with a razor-blade the skin sprang open and the jelly stuff inside squeezed out as easily as you could wish.

4. Rewrite the passage replacing all the verbs you have identified with a verb of similar meaning.

Adjectives
In this task you will look at adjectives and consider how they can be used to create a vivid description.

5. Identify as many adjectives as you can in the following passages from 'Mrs Bixby and the Colonel's Coat':

At first she thought it *was* black; but when she held it closer to the window she saw that there was a touch of blue in it as well, a deep rich blue, like cobalt. Quickly she looked at the label. It said simply, WILD LABRADOR MINK.

Quickly she slipped off her own plain red coat. She was panting a little now, she couldn't help it, and her eyes were stretched very wide. But oh God, the feel of that fur! And those huge wide sleeves with their thick turned-up cuffs. Who was it had once told her that they always used female skins for the arms and male skins for the rest of the coat?

6. Write a description of one of your favourite belongings. It may be a special present you received for a birthday or Christmas. Try to convey to the reader how special it is and how you felt when it came into your possession for the first time. Use as many interesting and relevant adjectives as you can think of.

Creating atmosphere 1: calm

In this task you are going to examine Roald Dahl's imaginative and varied use of nouns, adjectives and verbs to create an atmosphere of calm and relaxation.

7. Create three columns in your exercise book using the headings *Nouns*, *Adjectives* and *Verbs*. Carefully read the following passage from 'Man from the South' and write down all the nouns, adjectives and verbs which help to create the desired atmosphere. Put your words in the appropriate column.

It was a fine garden with lawns and beds of azaleas and tall coconut palms, and the wind was blowing strongly through the tops of the palm trees, making the leaves hiss and crackle as though they were on fire. I could see the clusters of the big brown nuts hanging down underneath the leaves.

There were plenty of deck-chairs around the swimming pool and there were white tables and huge brightly coloured umbrellas and sunburned men and women sitting around in bathing suits. In the pool itself there were three or four girls and about a dozen boys, all splashing about and making a lot of noise and throwing a large rubber ball at one another.

8. Imagine a holiday location, or any place you know well, and describe how it looks and feels in the summer. Think about:

- nouns, adjectives and verbs
- how people behave differently at different times of the year
- differences in atmosphere caused by changes in the weather.

Describe how it might appear in the winter.

Creating atmosphere 2: tension

In this task you are going to examine Dahl's imaginative and varied use of words and phrases to create an atmosphere of tension and fear.

9. Read carefully the following passage from 'The Ratcatcher' and write down all the words and phrases which help to create the tense atmosphere. Pick five words or phrases, and comment on why they are effective in creating the desired effect.

At this point, the ratman again began to move his face closer. Very slowly he did it, so slowly there wasn't any movement to be seen at all except that the face just happened to be a fraction closer each time you looked. He never took his eyes from the rat. The tension was considerable and I wanted suddenly to cry out and tell him to stop. I wanted him to stop because it was making me feel sick inside, but I couldn't bring myself to say the word. Something extremely unpleasant was about to happen – I was sure of that. Something sinister and cruel and ratlike, and perhaps it really would make me sick. But I had to see it now.

10. Describe an incident that is frightening or has a great deal of tension. It could involve a hunter stalking his or her prey, or a person being following late at night.

Similes

A simile is a comparison using *like* or *as*. Writers use them to create an interesting image in the reader's mind, for example:

- she was *like* an angel
- she was as beautiful *as* an angel.

In this task you will look at the use of similes in 'The Landlady' and consider how Dahl uses them to create an interesting picture in the mind's eye of the reader.

11. Look at the following similes from 'The Landlady'. Write down what each one means and then comment on the ideas and feelings Roald Dahl is trying to put in the reader's mind. How effective is each simile?

   a) 'the wind was like a flat blade of ice on his cheeks'
   b) 'Each word was like a large black eye staring at him through the glass.'
   c) 'But this dame was like a jack-in-the-box.'
   d) 'She looked exactly like the mother of one's best school friend welcoming one into the house to stay for the Christmas holidays.'
   e) 'he turned and saw his landlady sailing into the room with a large silver tea tray in her hands. She was holding it well out in front of her, and rather high up, as though the tray were a pair of reins on a frisky horse.'

12. Write a description of a person you know well using as many imaginative similes as you can think of. Try to make them as inventive as Roald Dahl's.

Speech

In this task you will look at how to set out speech and punctuate it correctly. You will also consider the use of the word 'said'.

13. Examine passages from the stories which include dialogue and the use of speech marks. Work out when you need speech marks. Ask yourself:

   - What words are actually contained in the speech marks?
   - What other punctuation is being used?
   - When is a new line needed?

14. Write out the following passage putting in all the correct punctuation:

I don't want it he said
She moved uneasily in her chair, the large eyes still watching his face But you *must* have supper I can easily do it here I'd like

to do it We can have lamb chops Or pork Anything you want
Everything's in the freezer

Forget it he said

But darling you *must* eat I'll fix it anyway and then you can
have it or not as you like

She stood up and placed her sewing on the table by the lamp

Sit down he said Just for a minute sit down

It wasn't till then that she began to get frightened

Go on he said Sit down

15. What words could be used instead of 'said'? Why do you
think Roald Dahl keeps using 'said' rather than varying his
vocabulary?

Text

Use words and phrases from the text to support your ideas in the
following tasks.

1. Write about Roald Dahl's use of twists and turns in two of the
   stories in this selection (for example, 'Man from the South' and
   'The Landlady'). Think about:

   • unusual, unexpected or dramatic events
   • how Dahl builds up feelings of tension, fear and
     expectation
   • the actions and speech of characters
   • clues in the description of people and places
   • changes in atmosphere and mood
   • Dahl's use of language.

2. Many of Roald Dahl's stories reflect a love of the bizarre and
   include strange and weird characters (for example, ratcatchers,
   fingersmiths, taxidermists, tattooists). Write about two of his
   more unusual characters you have enjoyed reading about in
   this selection. Look at:

   • your character's actions, mannerisms and speech
   • what other characters in the stories think of them

- your response to them as a reader
- the language used to describe them.

3. Roald Dahl portrays many of his female characters in a very unfavourable light. Write about two of the female characters in this selection commenting on their similarities and differences. Think about:

- each character's actions, mannerisms and speech
- what other characters in the stories think of them
- your response to them as a reader
- the language used to describe them
- the writer's attitude towards them.

Find female characters in other Roald Dahl stories, not included in this selection, who portray unpleasant characteristics.

4. Compare the story 'Galloping Foxley' and the chapter 'Fagging' from Roald Dahl's autobiographical book *Boy* (Puffin, 1995). Look at:

- the events in the story
- Dahl's use of language
- his attitude towards his school days.

5. Many of these stories have been filmed for a television series, *Tales of the Unexpected*. Write a television/film script for one of these stories, including descriptions of setting, directions for actors, sound effects, music, the casting of characters, lighting and camera angles.

In your script, write a different ending from the one Roald Dahl used in his story.

6. Examine one of the following themes taken from the stories in this selection: gambling, breaking the law, taking risks, poaching, horror, corrupt authority, violence, death. Write about how Roald Dahl treats your chosen theme in at least two of the stories in this selection. Does your chosen theme appear in any other of Roald Dahl's stories?

7. Compare Roald Dahl's short story 'Mrs Bixby and the Colonel's Coat' with Guy de Maupassant's 'The Necklace' (*Twisters*, Longman 2000). Look for similarities and differences.

Write about:

- unusual twists and turns
- the moods of the central characters at different stages of the stories
- themes, particularly greed and vanity
- the actions and speech of the characters, especially that of the women
- the attitude of each husband towards his wife
- descriptions of people and places
- changes in atmosphere and the build up of tension in each story
- both writers' use of language and imagery
- the ending of each story.

8. Compare one of the stories in this selection with a short story written by another author. Consider the following:

- unusual, unexpected or dramatic events
- atmosphere and moods
- themes
- the actions and speech of characters
- descriptions of people and places
- changes in atmosphere and mood
- devices and techniques used by each writer
- both writers' use of language and imagery.

Glossary

Lamb to the Slaughter
27   **translucent:** shining
28   **luxuriate:** enjoy with great pleasure
36   **exasperated:** irritated

The Landlady
42   **façades:** house fronts
42   **rapacious:** greedy
43   **compulsion:** desire
48   **Dempsey and Tunney:** famous boxers
48   **Churchill and Roosevelt:** political leaders
49   **emanate:** flow
50   **blemish:** mark

The Champion of the World
62   **seconal:** sleeping pill
63   **debilitated:** weak and infirm
69   **fraternity:** group or society
79   **partial:** fond of
79   **proprietary air:** superior, as if he owned her

Galloping Foxley
85   **commuting:** travelling to and from work
85   **disclamatory:** rejecting
85   **protestant:** protesting
86   **perambulation:** walk
86   **pince-nez:** glasses perched on the end of the nose
86   **sedulous:** hard working
86   **exhortation:** encouragement
87   **over-complacent:** too self-satisfied
89   **lasciviously:** indecently
89   **salacious:** lustful

91	**impinging:** encroaching or forcing upon
95	**invariably:** nearly always
95	**excruciating:** very painful
96	**impudent:** cheeky

Mrs Bixby and the Colonel's Coat

103	**parlay:** double up, increase
104	**cuckold:** a man whose wife has been unfaithful
106	**ministrations:** attentions
107	**voluptuous:** sexually attractive, having a full figure
108	**canals, bicuspids and caries:** technical dental terms
113	**prognathous:** projecting
113	**caricature:** picture in which features are exaggerated
113	**Sam Weller:** Dickens character
113	**Beau Brummel:** famous early nineteenth-century man of fashion
113	**masquerade:** pretence
113	**Lewis Carroll:** author of *Alice in Wonderland*
114	**inlays:** gold fillings
116	**magnanimously:** generously
120	**mangy:** scruffy

Skin

123	**Chaim Soutine:** Russian painter who lived in Paris
123	**Kalmuck:** a person from Mongolia – used here as a nickname
133	**impasto:** painting with thick heavy layers
134	**Le Havre:** port in northern France
135	**collops:** slices of meat
136	**flunkey:** assistant
140	**Chambertin:** famous French wine

The Ratcatcher

| 150 | **surreptitious:** with stealth |
| 154 | **shilling:** five pence (pre-decimal: 12 old pennies) |

Title list

0 582 25401 9	Poems 2	

Post-1914 Plays

0 582 30242 0	Absent Friends	Alan Ayckbourn
0 582 06019 2	The Winslow Boy	Terrence Rattigan
0 582 22389 X	P'Tang, Yang, Kipperbang & other TV plays	Jack Rosenthal
0 582 43445 9	Educating Rita	Willy Russell
0 582 08173 4	Shirley Valentine	Willy Russell
0 582 25383 7	Ten Short Plays	
0 582 25394 2	Scenes from Plays	
0 582 06014 1	The Royal Hunt of the Sun	Peter Shaffer
0 582 09712 6	Equus	Peter Shaffer
0 582 06015 X	Pygmalion	Bernard Shaw
0 582 07786 9	Saint Joan	Bernard Shaw
0 582 25396 9	The Rivals/The School for Scandal	Richard Brinsley Sheridan

Post-1914 Stories from other Cultures

0 582 28730 8	Quartet of Stories	
0 582 06011 7	July's People	Nadine Gordimer
0 582 25398 5	Heat and Dust	Ruth Prawer Jhabvala
0 582 07787 7	Cry, the Beloved Country	Alan Paton
0 582 03922 3	Stories from Asia	
0 582 25393 4	Stories from Africa	
0 582 28929 7	Global Tales	

Post-1914 Non-Fiction

0 582 25391 8	Genres	
0 582 25384 5	Diaries and Letters	
0 582 28932 7	Introducing Media	
0 582 25386 1	Travel Writing	
0 582 08837 2	Autobiographies	
0 582 01736 X	The Diary of Anne Frank	

Pre-1914 Fiction

0 582 07720 6	Pride and Prejudice	Jane Austen
0 582 07719 2	Jane Eyre	Charlotte Brontë
0 582 07782 6	Wuthering Heights	Emily Brontë
0 582 07783 4	Great Expectations	Charles Dickens
0 582 28729 4	Oliver Twist	Charles Dickens
0 582 23664 9	A Christmas Carol	Charles Dickens
0 582 23662 2	Silas Marner	George Eliot
0 582 22586 8	The Mayor of Casterbridge	Thomas Hardy
0 582 07788 5	Far from the Madding Crowd	Thomas Hardy
0 582 30244 7	Ethan Frome	Edith Wharton

Pre-1914 Collections

0 582 25405 1	Wessex Tales	Thomas Hardy
0 582 28931 9	Stories Old and New	
0 582 28927 0	War Stories	
0 582 25388 8	Characters from Pre-20th Century Novels	
0 582 25384 5	Diaries and Letters	
0 582 25385 3	Highlights from 19th Century Novels	
0 582 25389 6	Landmarks	
0 582 25386 1	Travel Writing	
0 582 33807 7	19th Century Short Stories of Passion & Mystery	

Pre-1914 Poetry

0 582 22585 X	Poems from Other Centuries

Pre-1914 Plays

0 582 25397 7	She Stoops to Conquer	Oliver Goldsmith
0 582 24948 1	Three Plays	Henrik Ibsen
0 582 25409 4	Doctor Faustus	Christopher Marlowe
0 582 28930 0	Starting Shakespeare	
0 582 43444 0	The Devil's Disciple	Bernard Shaw
0 582 07785 0	Arms and the Man	Bernard Shaw
0 582 28731 6	The Duchess of Malfi	John Webster
0 582 07784 2	The Importance of Being Earnest	Oscar Wilde

NEW CENTURY READERS

Post-1914 Contemporary Fiction

0 582 32847 0	Granny the Pag	Nina Bawden
0 582 29254 9	The Real Plato Jones	Nina Bawden
0 582 25395 0	A Question of Courage	Marjorie Darke
0 582 32845 4	Daughter of the Sea	Berlie Doherty
0 582 43455 6	The Snake Stone	Berlie Doherty
0 582 29262 X	My Family and other Natural Disasters	Josephine Feeney
0 582 31941 2	The Tulip Touch	Anne Fine
0 582 43452 1	Flour Babies	Anne Fine
0 582 29257 3	A Pack of Liars	Anne Fine
0 582 29258 1	The Book of the Banshee	Anne Fine
0 582 29261 1	Madame Doubtfire	Anne Fine
0 582 29251 4	Step by Wicked Step	Anne Fine
0 582 29260 3	Goggle Eyes	Anne Fine
0 582 29255 7	MapHead	Lesley Howarth

0 582 43453 X	A Northern Childhood	George Layton
0 582 32846 2	Lizzie's Leaving	Joan Lingard
0 582 31967 6	Night Fires	Joan Lingard
0 582 43456 4	Goodnight Mister Tom	Michelle Magorian
0 582 43451 3	Journey to Jo'burg	Beverley Naidoo
0 582 36419 1	Aquila	Andrew Norriss
0 582 29256 5	Along a Lonely Road	Catherine Sefton
0 582 46148 0	The Red Pony	John Steinbeck
0 582 31966 8	A Serpent's Tooth	Robert Swindells
0 582 31968 4	Follow a Shadow	Robert Swindells
0 582 31964 1	Urn Burial	Robert Westall

Post-1914 Poetry

0 582 25400 0	Poems 1
0 582 22587 6	Poems in my Earphone

Post-1914 Plays

0 582 43450 5	Mirad, a Boy from Bosnia	Ad de Bont
0 582 09556 5	Bill's New Frock	Anne Fine
0 582 09555 7	Collision Course	Nigel Hinton
0 582 09554 9	Maid Marian and her Merry Men	Tony Robinson
0 582 10156 5	The Fwog Prince	Kaye Umansky

Pre-1914

0 582 42944 7	Oliver Twist	Charles Dickens
0 582 29253 0	Twisters	